The Passion of Muhammad Shakir

by

Guillermo Bosch

Published November, 2012
Fallen Bros. Press
6010 South Pacific Coast Highway #9
Redondo Beach CA 90277
ISBN: 78-0615763095 (Fallen Bros. Press)

Author's note: *"The Passion of Muhammad Shakir" was inspired by news reports and photographs of actual events. The story itself is, however, a fable, and not intended to be a documentary of persons living or dead. The characters and situations are solely the products of the author's imagination.*

For all those known
and unknown who have died
from humankind's inhumanity
to human beings.

CONTENTS .... Page

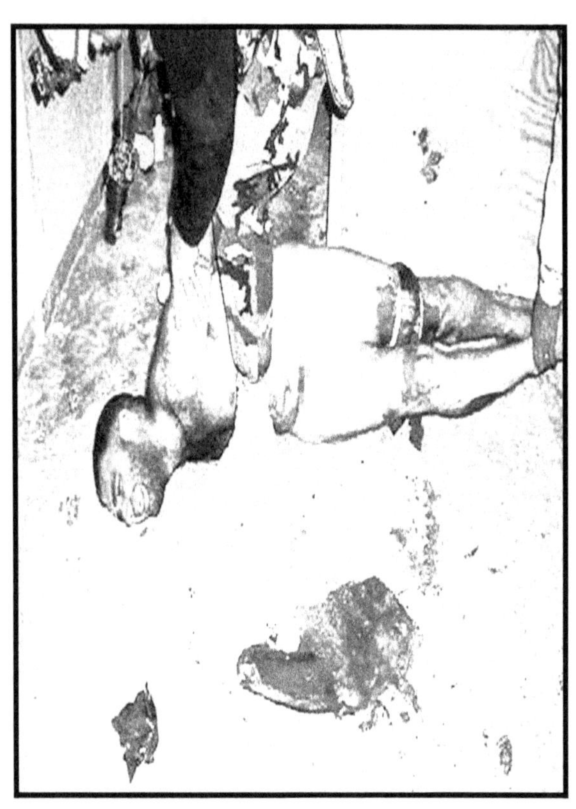

The First Day
The Awakening...

God is great. All praise is due to God, Who created the heavens and the earth and made the day and the night. Through Him, and in Him and with Him, I am...

And without Him, I am not.

God is my salvation, and if God wills it, He will bring me out of this darkness into His Light. There is no God but God. Praise God.

But my poor head pounds; my face is on fire. My eyes are open, but my head is covered and I cannot see anything but the dark cloth that covers me! My hands are bound behind my back. My legs are tied together. My feet have no feeling. Where am I? Why am I here?

I have no memory about how I came to be tied like a goat for slaughter. I do not know who wants to slit my throat and place me upon an unknown altar. Still, I am not afraid of death because I walk with my One True God.

Yet...yet...I do not understand because, if I walk with God, then why have I been hurled beneath the earth, to this devil's place, into this hell. Have I not been faithful to my God? I need to remember.

The air in this place stinks! What are those smells? Piss, yes, and shit. But also sulfur. Something is burning. I am sure of that. My stomach growls. It wants me to eat. Ha! Shut up, stupid stomach. I do not think you want me to eat what I smell!

Yes, yes, this must be hell. I must have committed a great, unknown sin, a sin I cannot remember. I am lost! God is great, but He has abandoned me. Still, I will remain faithful to Him.

Ah, my hands. If only they were free. Then I could scratch this cursed itch above my chin.

The floor is cold…cold and hard. But hell cannot be cold. If anything is real, this floor is real. This cold hard floor is not hell's floor. Maybe, I am not in hell, God willing. I am in some earthly place. But where?

I hear voices…near me, but not next to me. I am not alone? I try to speak, but my mouth is sealed. Ah, that is why I have such an itch.

My feet. Can I move my feet? No. There is no feeling in my feet. Can I move at all? A little. Along the floor, the cold hard floor, rough…stone, tile…concrete? Yes. Concrete. I can wiggle on the floor like a worm across the sand after the winter storms raise the river over its banks, like a happy little worm after the spring floods. Ha…wiggle, wiggle little worm.

I hear voices again. Some speak in my language, but others speak in the language of the crusaders. Ah…there is a memory… crusaders. Now I have two memories—worms after the desert rains and crusaders, crusaders with their bombs and their guns and their planes and their helicopters killing night and day. If I am in the place of the crusaders, if I am in a crusader cage, then I am in hell after all.

But why would the crusaders want me? I am a simple man. At least I think I am, but what am I?

Ah, another memory. I work with my hands. I am a…all I can remember is I work with my hands. And I am faithful to my God. I am, yes I am those things so I must be a simple man…not a man of words, or deep thoughts, not a teacher or a preacher, a simple man who works with his hands. Maybe a carpenter! I think I remember now: I am a humble carpenter! What would these people want with me?

Now I hear the voices of my people screaming, screaming in words I understand, "God is great. There is no God but God." And then there's a thump…a thud…low moaning…whispers, whispers in the language of the crusaders…laughter…a terrifying scream…silence.

Then the sound of their boots shuffling, louder and louder, shuffling toward me, and the whispering and laughter, toward me. I do not want to wiggle. I am not a worm. I am a nothing, a dry palm frond lying on the floor. I will not move…

I hear the sound of metal on metal, and then the creak of a door opening. The boots are near, very near. God willing, I will not tremble. I am still, silent, unmoving.

The man begs for the screaming to stop.

Stop screaming!

He hopes someone will help that wretched soul, but he also needs peace and quiet because he doesn't feel very good himself. In fact, he feels terrible.

My God, what happened to me? Am I dead?

If I am already dead, can I then ask myself if

I am dead?

I do not know. I have never been dead before. Hey you, stop screaming!

Ah! But wait…if I know someone is screaming, that means I can hear.

Good, good… what else can I hear?

Nothing else. Only this terrible screaming. But I can hear. So I am not dead.

And I am breathing.

My lungs fill up with air. They push the old air out, and they bring new air inside.

I am breathing!

Ah! And something is covering my mouth, so I am breathing through my nose. So…can I smell?

I will try to smell…

And the man really does try…sniff, sniff, sniffing like a newborn puppy searching for its mommy's teat, his nose searching the air…sniff, sniff, sniffing…

Yes! I do smell something. Phew! Ugh! It stinks!

Like rotting eggs and slaughtered sheep. Like cat piss and goat turds.

But I can smell.

Can I open my eyes?

Yes, I can open my eyes.

But I cannot see anything. No wait.

Hmmm. Ah! I can see.

My face is covered. But I can see. My tongue.

My tongue is moving inside my mouth. I will bite down. Hard.

Harder!

Ah. I taste blood. I can taste.

Do I feel anything?

Yes. My face itches and burns.

If only I could scratch…my face. I need to scratch my face!

The man's body strains, shudders and shakes, then collapses and becomes still again.

No. I cannot move my arms… I cannot move my hands… I cannot move my legs…

So…I can hear, see, smell taste, feel.

And I can think. That is important. I can think.

Or, at least I am thinking I think I can think. Ah, yes, well, I guess if I think I am thinking, then I am thinking. Ha!

The man's body twitches slightly again.

But I still have no memory. None.

I do not remember anything that happened before right now.

Maybe if I concentrate. I cannot.

Not with that awful screaming ringing in my ears.

And it grows louder. I am afraid.

The stench smells stronger. I am afraid.

I taste the blood in my mouth more sharply. I am in pain!

I must have been in an accident, yes, a serious accident. That must have been what happened…an accident, yes, and…

I think I do not want to know anymore. Not right now.

The man allows himself to slip away into unconsciousness. There is no more twitching from his trussed up body which lies on the cold concrete in a corner tight up against cinder block walls as the first morning light illuminates a fat, long-tailed rat which makes its way across the floor before it stops and flicks out it's tongue to capture a few grains of the crusted blood pooled near the man's head.

The First Memory
The Promise...

That man lying in his own blood on the hard concrete floor is named Muhammad, after the Prophet, last name: Shakir. He was born in a small town nestled alongside Al Furatan, the great central river.

Muhammad's mother's name is Marium. His father's name was Yusuf. Muhammad is thirty-three years old.

Twenty-eight years earlier. Muhammad, a small, wiry boy with intense, almost black eyes, and his almond-eyed, curly-haired friend Hakim are playing hide-and-seek in the cattail marshes along the river bank when, during a break in their play, Hakim, the taller and heavier of the two, says to Muhammad:

"I heard my mother and father say that you are a bastard."

Muhammad is angry, "I am not a bastard!" although neither he nor Hakim know the meaning of the word, but both sense that whatever the word means, it is not a good thing to be called a bastard. This does not concern Hakim. He senses yet another opportunity to lord it over Muhammad, so he presses on: "Yes you are. You are so a bastard." So Muhammad rolls his fists and flails his arms in the air as he rushes toward

Hakim. Hakim waits patiently, then punches Muhammad in the nose. Blood pours from Muhammad's nostrils. He is crying as he runs away, back toward the town. From that day on, Muhammad and Hakim are no longer friends.

A few weeks later, Muhammad is sitting by himself behind the stones of a collapsed wall studying the thousands of ants marching in disciplined columns from underneath the fallen stones when he overhears the town's dark-veiled hens cackling among themselves as they gather water from a neighborhood well. He hears his name, his mother's name and his father's name. He listens more closely. One wizened old woman points a crooked finger in the air and says: "Sister's…Old Yusuf 's rod is soft as butter. He could not have made that child!"

Another, short and squat, says: "And how would you know about Yusuf 's rod?"

The old woman takes up the challenge: "I knew it well for many years, and when last I touched that drooping member it was already more river roe than rod."

The others laugh.

"Maybe the boy is a prophet…his birth, a miracle," says the butcher's wife, a thin young woman given to religious visions.

The old woman spits in the dust. "The only miracle is that old Yusuf can keep a hold on such a young wife."

Muhammad remains hidden, but he listens as he squashes the ants with the tips of his fingers one by one until the scouts sent word back to the colony and the remaining soldiers choose a new path out from under a different rock away from Muhammad.

The following spring, during the Holy Days, after the rains

stop but before the searing sun-baked days of summer, Yusuf and Marium take the young Muhammad on a pilgrimage to the Holy Cities.

They walk. Short, thin, gray-bearded Yusuf in his skull cap and threadbare tan jacket. Marium in her black abaya and veil which only reveals her intense, curious eyes and a hint of the outlines of her generous curves. And Muhammad, dressed in a green tunic.

As they trudge along the road, they are enveloped by the dung-colored dust raised by the buses and trucks and taxis and sandals and bare feet of thousands upon thousands of pilgrims, so many, many people, all heading toward the Holy Cities, some chanting, some laughing, some silent in deep meditation as the afternoon sun burns orange filtered through those dust clouds carried along by a dry wind that blows across the arid fields.

Suddenly, the pace of the marchers quickens when in the distance they see the towers of the Great Place of Prayer in the Holiest of the Holy Cities—the Shrine to the Son-in-law of the Prophet, and as they approach, the crowds become so thick that Yusuf is forced to lift Muhammad up onto his shoulders as they walk through the narrow streets made even more narrow by the stands of the vendors hawking roasted lamb, millet, olives, onions…and books, hundreds and hundreds of books with green and brown and black and tan covers scattered across tables, sitting on shelves…and multicolored sashes and scarves and arm bands with black and green and red script proclaiming the Holy Words of the faithful…all of this magnificent and glorious and wonderful to a small boy from the countryside.

Yusuf brings Muhammad and Marium to a specific book

stall where a tall, thin young man with hooded eyes sits and smokes a cigarette as he studies the crowd. Yusuf peruses the different volumes and then makes a selection. The book's cover is dark green with gold lettering and reads: "Poetic Thoughts on Family Piety and Communal Morality."

Yusuf offers a price for the book. The thin man shakes his head. They haggle while Muhammad squats on the ground next to his mother. He leans into her and feels the comfort of her breast. He smiles when she drapes her arm on his shoulder. He presses his cheek against her thigh. Yusuf and the book seller agree on a price.

Yusuf is happy. They stop at another market stall and Yusuf chooses a roll of black cotton cloth which he presents to Marium so she can, as he says, fashion a new abaya for herself and a smaller smock for Muhammad. She bows respectfully, lowering her eyes, but she does not take the material. Instead she points to a length of blue cloth—soft blue like the morning desert sky. Yusuf hesitates. He thinks. But he is happy so he returns the black to the merchant and presents Marium with the blue she desires. Again she bows, but she allows her eyes to remain fixed on Yusuf to let him know he has made her happy. He is pleased, but embarrassed by her look and so he turns away.

The little family makes one more stop. Yusuf buys, without haggling, a green sash which he ties around Muhammad's forehead. He beams. He says: "The words written here, and now placed upon your head shall inspire you, my son, to greatness in all things."

Now Muhammad is happy. Yusuf has called him "his son." Muhammad reaches out for Yusuf 's hand as Yusuf picks him up and again carries him on his shoulders.

Marium says she is tired and dusty and needs to rest, She asks where they will stay the night since Yusuf has neglected to make plans for them.

Yusuf approaches guest house after guest house, but there are no rooms in the inns. Yusuf 's confidence sinks. His mood grows dark. Marium suggests they can stay at the house of a man from another tribe who has married her mother's cousin's cousin. The family now lives on the outskirts of the Holy City.

When they arrive at the cousin's house, they are greeted with many hugs and many kisses, but the cousin's house is filled with pilgrims from the husband's family. He says that Yusuf, Marium and Muhammad can stay in his stable with his one skinny cow and five goats. The cow stares at Muhammad with her sad brown eyes, and the goats have black and white spots. They are young and frisky and they chase after Muhammad when he runs past their pen. Marium curls up in the hay and falls asleep. Yusuf sits with his back against a rough wooden post reading from his new book.

That evening Yusuf and Muhammad leave Marium behind when they go to pray at the Holiest of All Holy shrines. Muhammad's eyes open wide. He stares in awe at the golden dome flanked by two golden towers. He sees a main gate taller than ten men, and after he enters, he observes that the walls of the central courtyard are inlaid with bright blue, rich golden and stark white mosaic tiles in patterns so complex they send his mind spinning. The courtyard is paved in stone, and the sanctuary covered with carpets softer than spring grass under his naked little feet. Just before the call to prayer, Yusuf brings Muhammad before a group of men wearing black turbans and flowing white robes who are arguing among themselves about the meaning of a passage from the Holy Book. The oldest, an imam with a white beard which had grown the length of his chest and ends atop a very generous belly, stops arguing and looks down at Muhammad. His fierce eyes bore into Muhammad, but Muhammad stares right back at him.

The imam holds up his hand to stop debate. Then he turns and asks Muhammad his name.

Muhammad answers: "Muhammad, son of Yusuf "

Then the imam asks him if he knows what is written on the sash tied around his head. Muhammad is confident. "A text from the Prophets: Every soul must taste of death…" His stare continues to hold the imam whose eyes search inside the boy's soul. The bearded man cocks his head to the left. "And what do you think of those words, Muhammad, son of Yusuf?"

Muhammad answers, "I am…I am not afraid to die!"

The Imam laughs scornfully. "Little boys are never afraid to die." But the words say, "to taste of death. What does it mean to taste of death and yet not die?"

Muhammad answers: "If one tastes of death and lives, one does not fear death which opens the Holy Path to life."

The Imam is startled. The others nod in approval. The Imam turns toward Yusuf. "Be proud, father. This child is wise beyond his years."

At that very moment, the muezzin's voice calls everyone to evening prayers. As Muhammad kneels next to Yusuf facing the City of the Tomb and they bow their heads then rise in supplication, Muhammad imagines living with the spirits of the Prophets and Poets and True Believers in the City of God. He dreams he sits before a golden altar, seated at the right hand of God—an old man who looks remarkably like the imam of the shrine.

After prayers Yusuf and Muhammad wander through the streets of the Holy City watching the marching men swinging chains that ching! ching! ching! when the men slam them against each other or onto the ground. Some men bare their backs and beat themselves with leather whips which raise angry welts and even open wounds. Other men carry swords which they use to slap the tops of their heads and cut themselves. Blood streams down their cheeks and becomes matted in their thick black beards.

And from everyone, from the marchers and from those who watch, there is chanting and shouts of praise to God and proclamations of faith and declarations of repentance for sins and transgressions against the words of the Holy Book. Muhammad looks up at Yusuf and sees that the old man's eyes are closed, his head raised toward the heavens. Yusuf 's lips move in fits and starts, mouthing words Muhammad cannot hear. And as Yusuf fervently prays, his hand squeezes Muhammad's so tightly Muhammad screams. Yusuf misinterprets Muhammad's screams as evidence of the child's own fervor because he lifts Muhammad up and with every last drop of his waning strength tosses Muhammad high into the air and the other men shout, "Praise God," as they reach out to catch Muhammad and set him down gently when he falls back to earth.

Later, as Muhammad and Yusuf, both exhausted, walk together in the direction of the stable, Muhammad knows he has experienced the purest, true freedom one can experience, and despite the smoke and dust, the air Muhammad breaths is crystal clear, and despite the constant noise Muhammad only hears the sound of silence, and all remaining fear passes from him.

Then, as they approach the stable , Yusuf stops abruptly. His hand again tightly grips Muhammad's who hears a sound he had never heard before although he immediately knows what that sound is—his mother laughing! Suddenly Yusuf is running, dragging Muhammad behind him as they charge inside the stable where Marium sits on a mound of straw, her veil lowered, her naked ankles exposed, talking to a handsome young man who wears rimless glasses and a black silk turban.

Yusuf is enraged. He moves forward, his fist in the air, but the young man jumps up, grabs Yusuf's arm and wrestles him to the ground. The young man stands over Yusuf. Yusuf is on his knees before the younger man…In front of Marium.

Muhammad runs into his mother's arms and she presses his head against her breast. She points to the man in the turban and speaks to her husband, "Yusuf, this man did nothing," she cries. But her words cannot calm Yusuf. He struggles to rise, but each time the young man forces him back onto his knees.

Marium is crying. "Go away," she says to the young man. He looks at her. "Please, just go," she pleads.

The young man releases Yusuf and walks away. Yusuf collapses onto the stable floor. He is crying, and Muhammad had never seen Yusuf cry. In one night he has seen his mother laugh, Yusuf cry.

Then Yusuf slowly pulls himself up. He refuses to look at Marium or Muhammad while he walks over to where his gift of the beautiful blue cloth is lying. Marium says: " He is my cousin, Yusuf. He is only my cousin."

Yusuf is not listening. He picks up the cloth, and without speaking another word, his head low, his shoulders drooped, stumbles out of the stable.

When Marium sees Yusuf leave looking like a man even older than he is, Marium stops crying and begins to moan, rocking back and forth in her anguish. She pulls open her abaya and exposes her breast to Muhammad's lips. He takes her nipple and sucks eagerly as they sway back and forth together in their pain. And their misery. And their pleasure. And Muhammad falls asleep with his mouth on Marium's breast.

In the morning, when the rooster crows three times, Muhammad awakens. He sees his mother sleeping next to him. He sees the skinny cow's brown eyes staring at him. He hears the black and white goats jumping and kicking against the side of their stall. He smells the hay.

The rooster crows again. Marium opens her eyes. She looks at Muhammad. Then she looks down at herself and quickly drapes her abaya over her body and grabs hold of her son's hand.

The two of them walk out into the early morning air. The birds are singing. The sky turns from gray to blue. There is a thin layer of dew over the dusty ground.

Muhammad looks up, and is amazed to see Yusuf flying under an almond tree growing in a small field across from the stable.

Muhammad says: "Look. Momma, Yusuf can fly."

"Yes, Muhammad, he is flying away, away from this world."

"Why is he leaving us, Momma? Is he mad at us?"

"Your father wants a different world."

Muhammad is angry. "He is not my father. I know your secret. He is not my father."

"But Muhammad, he is your father, may he rest in peace. I

swear to you on the Holy Book. He is your father."

And so Muhammad looks up at his father suspended in the sky, floating over Muhammad, his head slumped against his chest, the blue cloth wrapped around his neck melting into the blue of the morning sky as he twists and turns, his eyes wide open glaring down at his son and his wife.

Marium turns away and covers her face with her veil, but Muhammad keeps staring into the heavens, searching for the angels who will come to deliver his father into paradise.

The Second Day
Measuring Up...

There is movement from the body in the corner. The fat rat backs off and keeps its distance. It knows how to survive.

I arise from the fog. I like the sound of that. Rising from the fog…arising from the fog…he is risen! I am back.

But, nothing is clear.

Well, at least the screaming has stopped.

I really wish I could free my hands to scratch my face. The way it itches and burns. Pure torture. I have got to do something.

But I cannot move my arms, cannot move my legs. Why?

Was I paralyzed in the accident?

Come on. Try to move. Try to move.

Ah! Look at me! I can wiggle like a worm wiggles across the sand after the winter storms raise the river over its banks… wiggle like a happy little worm after the spring floods. Ha… wiggle, wiggle little worm. Ha, ha!

The man's body undulates across the floor, moving from the corner out toward the center of the room.

Whew! That was a lot of work for nothing. Where am I anyway?

This cannot be a hospital. No one has come to care for me. No one has even talked to me.

Maybe they think I am dead. Maybe they have dumped me in the basement to wait for my burial…

Oh no! That is what happened. That explains everything. I am wrapped in my burial shroud! That is why I cannot move. That is why my head is covered! No! No! They will put me in the ground and throw dirt over me, but I am alive! I am alive! Help! Help!

The man flops back and forth with surprising energy, driven by his instinct to survive, now more like a fish out of water than a worm.

His cries for help echo down the corridors where they are heard by those who have been waiting. Now they go to him.

Ah! Someone heard me! I hear voices…I hear footsteps running toward me…Oh yes, yes. I am saved!

Hey, hey, I am in here. I am here!

There is the sound of metal on metal, then the creak of a door opening.

Oh, yes, they have found me. I am so happy I will not be buried alive. Unwrap me, please. Set me free!

Two men enter the room.

The first is a middle-aged man, tall, very thin. He has closely cropped pure white hair, and he's clean shaven. He has steel gray eyes, a pale complexion. A jagged scar runs from his left ear across his cheek to the middle of his chin. He is dressed in full regulation combat gear. His cap shows his rank—captain.

The other man is short, stocky, has a dark complexion, wears a mustache, has brown eyes and a flat oval face pocked by serious bouts of acne from his teenage years. He also wears military combat uniform, although he's in his undershirt to show off his powerful chest and arm muscles. His tags hang from a metal chain outside the shirt and list his rank as a Pfc.

"What's it saying, soldier?"

"Hadji talk, sir. He's cursing us out, I imagine."

"What did you say, soldier?" "Sir?"

"Never refer to this bag of shit as 'he'. These are not people. They are vermin with one goal—to destroy our way of life. To destroy us. Is that clear, soldier?"

"Yes, sir!"

I move as much as I can. I call out to them. I want them to know I am alive!

But Aaaagh! What is this? Someone's boot kicks me in my kidneys. I feel like I have been cut open. My nerves tremble so.

Aaaagh! Again! Why? Why are they hurting me?

"So, what is this thing we have here, soldier?"

"A dangerous thing, sir. A real evil doer." "How long has it been here?"

"It was brought in last night, sir. From the west."

"It smells like crap."

"It has been burned, sir. On its face and arms."

"Burns? Then it should have treatment. Cool it off, soldier."

"Yes, sir!"

The younger man unzips his trousers and pisses on the body of the man lying on the floor.

"Yes, cool off this thing. It needs cooling."

Water, they are hosing me off...Ah! But no, this is not water. This is...piss! One of these fools is pissing on me!

The man's body tries to turn away from urine stream. The soldier finishes and zips up.

"Why is that one foot all crooked, soldier?" "I believe it's broken, sir."

"Broken. Well straighten it out for the poor hadji, soldier."

"Yes, sir."

Strong hands grip my foot...and then—thunder and lightening inside my head, inside my body, inside me and I hear myself scream, "Aaaagh! "

I am crying. I am so ashamed whimpering here on the floor like a stupid dog, my tail between my legs, begging for my master to stop beating me.

"So what's he packin' there, soldier?" "I don't know, sir."

The older man goes to the door and shouts down the corridor.

"Corporal, come on down here. We need to measure this thing. This thing's thing."

There is a lot of laughing from the end of the corridor. A few moments. Then a young woman appears in the doorway. She has short brown hair, a boyish, pixie-like face, freckles across her nose, a hint of sunburn on her cheeks, green eyes and a thin mouth. Her arms are muscled, her stomach tight, small breasts, combat trousers and a full t-shirt.

"The usual inch-and-a-half, sir?" "You tell me, Corporal."

She slaps on a pair of latex gloves, walks over to the man on the ground, lifts his tunic, loosens his trousers and studies his penis.

What are these idiots doing now? Why are they...Oh My God...they're going to castrate me...Oh My God...Oh My God...why have You forsaken me?

"Barely over an inch, sir!".

"Can't you make it bigger, Corporal?"

The woman giggles.

I hear a woman's voice laughing at me. They are going to have a woman castrate me? Then I feel her hands on me. Oh! I am so afraid…

And yet, I am a man. A poor helpless weak man, but still a man, and so I grow with each touch.

And then…she doesn't don't cut me. Instead, her hands move up and down my shaft, slowly at first, then as my blood fills my veins, more vigorously, and my hips thrust against the floor and my legs cramp. I call out: "Aaaagh! " but still her hands move faster and faster…

"It's alive. It's alive!"

And I grow more…and more. I cannot stop myself even though I know this growing is not a good thing, not now, not in this place, no, but I am a man, and my fluids rise up through my shaft toward the tip…

And then her hands squeeze my testes so hard my eyes are bursting and white stars shoot across my brain. My head bounces off the floor. And through my pain I hear their laughter as it breaks in waves across my broken body.

The woman giggles seductively. "It grew for awhile, sir. But I think I killed it."

"Good work, Corporal. That's enough for now. Come on…let's go have lunch."

There is hurt on every part of me. My testes throb, but they are still here, swollen below my shaft.

So…it is clear this is not a hospital. I am in trouble. Serious trouble. Something is terribly wrong. I do not know what to do…

The Second Memory
River Nymph...

After Yusuf's death, the child, Muhammad, and his mother Marium return to their town where they live in poverty and are shunned by all except the men who come to offer Marium a place in their household as the second, third or fourth wife. But she always refuses, prefer- ring instead to be the first wife of a dead man. As his father had wished, Muhammad is enrolled in a religious school even though most of the other boys in the town attend the government school. They study the words of men who control money, power and politics. Muhammad studies the Word of God.

The Imam of Muhammad's religious school, Ali Mansur Al-Wahim, is a not the fierce old man one might imagine, but a huge gentle giant who so loves the Word that he inspires his students to become Poets of the Book, and all of them can recite, in cadence and from memory, the major chapters of The Book, such is their devotion. But Imam Al-Wahim also teases them with riddles and practical jokes, and his great booming laughter shakes the walls of their simple classroom.

"A devout and faithful farmer is sent to prison for making the Holy Pilgrimage," says Imam Ali, "and so his poor wife is forced to try and work the land to keep their children from starving." The imam bows his head as if in deep thought.

Then he continues: "But the woman has never plowed a field, so she decides to send a message to her husband in which she begs him to tell her the best time to plant." The imam gazes around his little group to make sure they are all listening.

"So," says the imam, warming to his story, "being a good husband even though he is being kept in prison, he sends a message back to his wife: 'My dearest wife, you must go to your father and borrow money to feed our children. Do not go near our field for that is where the guns are buried.'" The imam's eyes grow wide at the mention of guns, and his boys exclaim in oooo's and aaaah's.

Then Imam Ali raises his hands to quiet them. "Now, when the prison censors read the farmer's message, they sent soldiers to the field where they dug furiously for three days and three nights looking for the guns, but they didn't find one single, solitary weapon." Imam Ali's face expresses the total frustration and confusion of the soldiers.

"After the soldiers left, the farmer sent another message to his wife." The imam keeps them in suspense for the count of three. "The new message said: 'Now is the time to plant our field.'"

The Imam is silent for a moment while the lesson of the joke sinks in. Then he explodes with a great roar and the boys also begin laughing so loud the students in the nearby government school believe, at least for that moment, that they have made the wrong choice if religious students are having so much fun.

One day, as Muhammad walks home, reciting to himself

the passage he has chosen to memorize that day, he finds himself surrounded by a gang of boys from the government school which includes his childhood friend, Hakim. The boys taunt Muhammad with religious insults, then Hakim reopens old wounds, "He's no holy, rolly, polly boy, he's a bastard!"

Muhammad's face turns red. Seeing his reaction, the boys take up the chant: "Bastard…bastard…"

Muhammad explodes and tackles Hakim. The two boys end up scuffling on the ground while the other boys form a circle and yell encouragement to Hakim.

"Kick the bastard's butt, Hakim."

"Muhammad's mother's a whore!"

One boy steps forward and kicks Muhammad while he's on the ground.

"Where's your God now, sissy boy?" Suddenly the circle grows silent. Imam Ali's huge bear paws reach out and grab each of the fighters by his collar. The imam holds both boys in the air until they each calm down. When they do, Imam Ali returns Hakim to his friends and they run off. Then he confronts Muhammad.

"Why were you fighting?"

"They insulted God."

The Imam smiles. "I'm sure God appreciates your defense, Muhammad, but do you really believe God needs you to fight his battles?"

Muhammad quotes from The Book: "'Oh you who believe! When you meet those who disbelieve marching for war, then turn not your backs to them.'"

"'…Show them kindness and deal with them justly; surely God loves the doers of justice.'" Imam Ali replies.

Muhammad hesitates. Then he says, "But Imam, you have

not given me the entire quote: 'God does not forbid you respecting those who have not made war against you on account of religion, and have not driven you forth from your homes, that you show them kindness and deal with them justly; surely God loves the doers of justice.' And just as surely, God wants me to fight those who make war on our religion?"

Imam Ali laughs. "I have taught you too well."

He puts his hand on the boy's head and scruffs up Muhammad's hair.

Muhammad is pleased. "Well, Imam Ali, they also called me a bastard."

"Ho! Ha! So maybe this fight was not so much about going to war for God?"

"I also fought for my mother, Imam Ali, for her honor."

"I know your mother. She is a good and chaste woman."

"All my life I have heard bad things about her?"

"Listen , Muhammad. One day, one of Mullah Al-Din"s friends came over and wanted to borrow his donkey for a day or two. Mullah, knowing his friend, was not favorably inclined to the request, and came up with the excuse that someone had already borrowed his donkey.

Just as Mullah uttered these words, his donkey started braying in his backyard. Hearing the sound, his friend gave him an accusing look, to which Mullah replied: 'I refuse to have any further dealings with you since you take a donkey's word over mine.'"

Muhammad laughs.

"Pay attention to the donkey, Muhammad, not to those who want something from you." And so Muhammad grows from a boy to a young man under the teachings of Imam Ali and the love of his mother Marium. While one might argue this powerful combination of God and love creates an admirable human being, and Muhammad has become, demonstrably, an admirable human being, that nurturing also creates a boy who does not fit in easily with the others in his town.

By the time he is able to grow a wispy beard and mustache, Muhammad is a loner, a skinny young man given to wandering about the desert or taking long early morning walks along the river bank. He is a serious, somewhat mystical young man given to staring into the sun- bleached sky asking unanswerable questions and seeking nonexistent messages in the shapes and sizes of clouds.

One early morning, as he walks alongside the river studying a random camel-shaped cloud, Muhammad is astonished when he hears a splash followed by a delighted squeal. He turns his attention to the river and sees…

…A girl! A young girl. A girl just entering the age for bearing children. She rises out of the river, her long wet black hair clinging to her face and arms. She reaches up with both hands, arches her neck and pulls her hair back from her face. She remains like that, for a precious moment, letting the sun warm her body.

Muhammad is transfixed. He cannot think, He cannot move. He cannot breath.

Then the girl covers herself with her abaya, steps into her sandals and is gone.

But, once he has seen her, Muhammad can- not let her go. He returns to the same spot each day and hides among the reeds. Days pass. She does not return.

And then one day…she does.

He discovers that the girl bathes in that same place on the

same day at the same time each week, and he cannot, will not stop seeing her. And as he watches, he touches himself. Yes, he does. And more than once he releases his seed upon the ground. Yes, he does. And although he knows that to release his seed without it entering the body of a woman is a grave sin, he justifies his actions as young men often do by telling himself that at least he fertilized Mother Earth!

Unfortunately, unknown to Muhammad, he is not the only one who has caught site of the girl bathing in the river. Hakim, now a first-year recruit in the national police force, is also hiding in the reeds along with his buddies, watching the girl; and their lust is inflamed by their challenges to each other to be the one who conquers their unsuspecting prey.

On one particularly hot day, as Muhammad watches the girl and touches himself lightly suddenly Hakim and two others leap out of the reeds and run toward the girl. She tries to grab her abaya, but one of the attackers rips it out of her hands before she can dress. She tries to flee, but Hakim grabs her arm and he will not let her go.

Meanwhile, Muhammad gathers himself together and starts running toward the scene. He is screaming, "Leave her alone! Leave her alone!"

When Hakim and his friends see Muhammad, they release the girl and prepare to attack the skinny young man racing toward them. While Muhammad is able to absorb their initial blows, it's three against one, and Muhammad is quickly brought down. Muhammad shouts to the girl still struggling with her abaya, "Run…forget your clothes…run! Now!"

But the girl's sense of modesty forces her to be more concerned with covering her nakedness than escaping. And that is why Hakim has time to capture her again.

As he holds onto her, she struggles and momentarily escapes from his grasp. Hakim is at first annoyed, then excited by her resistance. Finally his desire overwhelms him. He throws the girl to the ground, pulls down his uniform trousers, spreads the girl's legs apart and brutally enters her. She, overcome by shame and pain, cannot even scream. She lies there passively until Hakim is finished with her, Then, Hakim helps restrain Muhammad, while the other two take their turns with the girl.

Hakim whispers in Muhammad's ear, taunting him, "Why doesn't God protect her, Muhammad? Tell me, why doesn't God protect her?"

Muhammad can only snivel in frustration. Snot pours from his nose and his eyes fill with tears.

"There will be vengeance," he vows.

Hakim laughs. "I am a policeman. If you or the girl say anything, anything at all, here's our story: We happened upon the scene when we heard the girl screaming. We saw you raping her. We stopped the crime but you ran away."

"We will tell the truth. The truth will prevail."

"The word of a religious fanatic believed against the testimony of a policeman? That will never happen."

"Some day it will."

"And the river will flow backwards into the mountains and the sun will rise in the west. You're pathetic, Muhammad. You'll always be a bastard. You'll never fit in."

With that, Hakim and the others sulk off, Muhammad hears the girl moaning. He pulls himself up out of the dirt and approaches her. "I tried…"

The girl buries her face in the sand and refuses to look at Muhammad.

Muhammad covers her with her abaya, lifts her limp body into his arms and carries her away from the scene of her devastation.

But he does not know where to take her. The decision is fraught with danger. If her rape is known, the girl's life, not the lives of those who violated her, is ruined. But she needs help. She cannot be abandoned.

And so he brings her to his mother, Marium. She takes the child, comforts her, cleans her body, soothes her troubled mind as best she can and calms her into sleep. Then she asks her son what happened, and after he tells her, she asks what he intends to do now.

"I do not know," says Muhammad. "That is why I came here."

"I can take care of her, my son, but I cannot advise you on the ways of the world. You must speak to Imam Ali. He will know the way forward."

The Imam listens to Muhammad's story without interruption or comment. Then he says: "You know, Muhammad, the prophet took a wife much, much younger. Is this girl old enough for marriage?"

"Yes. Barely, but yes."

"And you desire her…even now, after what happened?"

"Yes."

"Consider your answer, Muhammad. She has suffered greatly. This suffering will never leave her. She will always be very cautious, controlled, never really open to you even if you give her everything. It will take faith and love as great as that you hold for God to keep her. She will always want to be free."

"I can make her love me."

"You can try, and, God willing, you may succeed."

"You will perform the ceremony for us?" "Yes. Of course."

"Then I will marry her. She is my responsibility. I did not protect her. Now, no one will. Even her family will destroy her." Imam Ali thinks for a moment.

"Mullah Al-Din and his wife came home one day to find that someone had broken into their house. Everything was stolen.

"'It's all your fault,' said his wife, for you should have made sure that the house was locked before we left.'

"Al-Din's neighbors gathered, and also accused him.

"'You did not lock the windows,' said one. "'Why did you not expect this?' said another.

"'The locks were faulty and you did not replace them,' said a third.

"'Just a moment,' said Al-Din, 'surely I am not the only one to blame'?

"'Well, who should we blame?' they all shouted.

"'What about the thieves?' said Al-Din. 'Are they totally innocent?'"

Muhammad smiles. Imam Ali musses Muhammad's hair the way he did when Muhammad was still a boy.

"Go to her. Give everything. Expect little in return. May God smile on you."

"And on you," says Muhammad.

The Third Day
The Great Pyramid...

They have returned. I must control myself. No crying like a frightened baby. No whimpering like a beaten dog...

"How is our puss bucket doing this morning, soldier?"

"It sleeps; it mumbles; it's lips move, but it only speaks gibberish."

"That is not acceptable, soldier. It must be broken down. It must be made to talk to us. I know it knows, and I know it knows I know, and I know it will tell us what it knows we know it knows."

"Come again, sir?"

"Prepare this thing for interrogation, soldier. We'll make this goddam' scumbag talk!"

The captain leaves, and the private is left with his captive. The captive, still bound and hooded lies silently on the floor. The private kneels down next to the prisoner's body.

Now someone is touching me. What is he doing? If only he would remove this sack covering my head. If only I could see. Maybe then I could know what is going on here. Maybe I could even convince them I should not be in this place.

Ah, he is untying my legs. Yes! And now he is removing the bonds from around my hands. I know this will feel good. I can even scratch… Ah, this is good. This is my chance to make friends. This is going to be a good, good day.

"Aaagh!" No, it doesn't feel good! God, help me! My foot is throbbing! When I move my arms, the little needles become razor blades shooting out from my wrists cutting through my forearms, slicing my elbows, opening the nerves in my biceps, trembling my triceps, tightening my shoulders with unquenchable fire!

I need to be still, motionless, or I will surely loose consciousness…

The captain returns. The corporal is right behind him. They enter the cell just as the prisoner screams. They show no emotion.

"Lift this bloody-assed bitch up off the floor, soldier."

Now he is trying to lift me up. No! Don't make me move! I do not want to show weakness, but I hear myself begging… "Stop! In the Name of God, please stop!" He drops me back onto the cold concrete. My head bounces once. Exploding stars…

I will lie here completely still, fooling them, I am silent, quiet, a dried up palm frond…

"I cannot hold him… I mean it up, sir."

"Corporal! Please assist the private."

I smell the woman—the woman who touches me there and then squeezes my testes with her hands. But, but…no, No! I am growing again when she approaches me, when she touches me. No, please, my private friend, stay calm. Do not betray me!

"Well, whaddaya' know. It appears to desire your special touch, Corporal."

"Yes, sir. It does, sir. Do we need another measurement, sir?"

"You enjoy measuring, Corporal?"

"I enjoy getting these hadjis ready for you, sir. Whatever it takes."

" Yeah. Whatever it takes. So, corporal…help the private here carry this piece a' shit."

"Yes, sir"

"Bring it to the latrine with the other pieces a' shit."

"Yes, sir."

They lift me up, and I am being carried somewhere, each movement unbearable, each step bringing me closer to throwing up. I wish I could just pass out. "Aaagh!" Maybe they are taking me to the hospital. Maybe this will still be a good day after all.

The corporal and the private carry the prisoner as they follow behind The Captain down a long hallway past open cells and other prisoners.

Someone screams: *God is great! There is no God but God!*

Then there's a loud whack! Wood against flesh and bone. More groans, but no more shouts. No more calls to God.

Who was screaming? Why do we all call for God in a place like this? I fear God has abandoned us here.

The private slips, and he, the prisoner and The Corporal almost fall.

"Aaagh!" Be careful or I will die before we get wherever we're going.

The captain and his motley entourage enter a large holding area. There are a dozen other prisoners in the area, in various stages of injury. Their faces are blank. They stare at the ground. They are devoid of will or desire.

Ah, we have stopped. I smell others. I hear groaning. Yes! This must be the hospital. We must be in the waiting room. Thank you, God. I am sorry I said You have abandoned me.

The private and The Corporal let loose their prisoner. He

falls onto the floor, too wracked with suffering to even call out. His body quivers and shakes as each painful spasm travels through his central nervous system.

The captain positions himself in the center of the room and addresses the assembled prisoners and guards.

"Listen up, boys and girls. First of all, welcome to the game room. This is where we all have fun. Now, today we're going to do a little body painting. When the paintings are finished, then we will analyze our work so we can get...what?"

The gathering shouts back in unison: "Information!"

"That's right boys and girls. Information. Now, gathered around you are the…uh, canvases."

People are laughing. Is the speaker telling a joke? Ah, but if everyone is in a good mood, then nothing bad is going to happen.

"But, sir, where's the paint, sir?"

The captain pushes a large plastic pail forward with his right foot.

"Here's your paint, Soldiers. Sorry we only have one color…brown!"

Again, they are all laughing. This is good. Something must be funny.

"And it don't smell so great, but it sure will stick to the canvas! So, let's make some hadji art!"

Something is being rubbed into my clothes. Are they trying to soothe my wounds? Whew, whatever it is they're rubbing over me, it stinks! Now they're rubbing my arms, my neck. I call out: "Take off the hood! Rub my face. It itches so much! It burns! Take off my hood!" But someone smacks me through the bag on my head so I don't say anything else.

But the smell of this salve is terrible…Oh! No! This is not a salve. This is shit they're rubbing all over me. Shit! They're cover-

ing me with shit! "*No! No!*"

Again someone slaps me. Another kicks me in the stomach. I whimper like a dog.

"Excellent, boys and girls! I did not know we had such talented artists in our little group."

"OoooHaaa! OoooHaaa!"

"But we have one problem, soldiers. We don't have an audience for your most excellent work.

"Why don't we take pictures, sir!"

"A most excellent suggestion, private. Do you have your camera?"

"Yes indeed, sir."

"Well, then, let's remove their hoods and show the world the butt-ugly mugs of the shit people."

"OoooHaaa! OoooHaaa!"

The soldiers stand over each the prisoners and rip off their hoods.

Praise God, they took the bag off of my head! I cannot see anything! Am I blind after all? No, I see light, but my eyes will not open wide. Oh, okay. Now there are shapes, feet, legs. I look up. I can see men moving. My God what is that? There is a blinding flash right in front of my eyes! Now another. What new torture is this? Now I squint. I see…one of the guards walking around with a…a camera! He is taking pictures of this…of us! I look around. I see other bodies near me. Some are guards in uniform, but most look like me. And we are all covered in shit! We stare at each other…ashamed…afraid of each other…

"Boys and girls, boys and girls. What are we thinking? If we're taking pictures, shouldn't we clean up the hadjis for their photo op?"

"Yes, sir!"

One of the guards approaches me. He throws me on the ground, and strips off my tunic. Then my shirt. Then my pants. I am naked in front of everyone!

I try to cover myself. Then I see a female guard. I know she is the one. I know it. She waves mockingly. My organ stirs. Please, no. Please, no. I use both hands to hide what is happening. She smiles…

Then another guard picks up a hose and points it at me. Suddenly I am being sprayed with water. It is a mixed blessing. The crust of brown shit is being washing away. But the water is cold. Very cold. I am trembling. I am shaking, out of control. But at least my organ wilts under the cold and I do not need to cover my- self with both hands

Now I can move one hand to scratch my face which burns even under the cold water. I scratch…but now I feel something on my fingers. I look down. What is this? My skin? It is my skin. My skin is falling away from my face! What is wrong with me?

"Group photo…" "OoooHaaa!" "Group photo…" "OoooHaaa!"

"This puss bucket belongs on the bottom, soldier."

A guard drags me toward the middle of the floor. He lays me out on the ground. As he moves away he steps on my hand, crushing my fingers, and I scream as this new damage takes its toll. Hands broken, skin falling off of my face…what more can they do to me?

Much more.

"Have you ever seen pictures of the pyramids, boys and girls?"

"Yes, sir!"

"But have you ever been to Egypt?" "No, sir!"

"Then let's build a pyramid right here in Hadjiland so you

can see one in the flesh!"

"OoooHaaa!"

One of the guards positions another naked prisoner next to me, making sure the other prisoner's organ is up against my butt. The other prisoner quietly mutters an apology and I nod in acceptance of his words and the truth that there is nothing we can do.

Then another prisoner is placed on the floor with his organ up against the butt of the man next to me. Then another. Then another. All of us lie there with each other's organs against our butts. And the guards are laughing.

"Looks like we gotta' all-queer daisy chain goin' here, sir!"

The captain shouts: "That's what we got! Bunch a' hadji faggots."

"OoooHaaa1"

The guards stack more naked prisoners on top of the other prisoners. They make sure each man's organ is rubbing against the butts of those on the bottom. Then they stack more prisoners on top of that layer. Then one more layer.

Aaagh! The weight of all these bodies has opened the sores on my chest. Blood and yellow fluid flow out from under me. Ah, but at least I am not cold anymore.

The guards are prowling and howling like desert jackals. They grab the camera from each other like it was freshly slaughtered meat.

Why are they taking pictures? Who will they show them to?

I look up. The female stands in front of us making a sign with her fingers. And she's smiling. Another guard takes a picture of the female making that sign. What does it mean? Are they going to kill us? What do they want from us? What do they want from me?

"Corporal!" "Yes, sir!"

"Would you like to climb to the top of the Great Pyramid of Hadji?"

"Yes, I would, sir. Very much, sir!"

The female climbs over the naked bodies, digging the toes of her boots into bare flesh. With each of her steps, the men groan in agony but the guards are cheering as the female guard kneels at the top of the pile, smiling and laughing with her arms raised in the air as if she has won a great victory.

The captain grabs the camera and announces: "Caption on this one: First American Woman To Climb To The Top Of The Pyramid Of Hadji!"

"OoooHaaa! OoooHaaa!"

Then, suddenly one of the men in the pyramid yells, "God is Great," and the pile collapses, bodies falling everywhere and The Corporal is flying through the air. She lands on her head with a thud! right next to the prisoner she had been torturing. She opens her eyes. She is dazed and confused as she blinks, then finds herself staring directly into Muhammad's face.

The female is lying in front of me, I want her. I do. Forgive me. I stretch forward and place my bloody, cracked lips upon her soft, smooth, pink ones. I let the tip of my tongue flick across her mouth. Forgive me. She closes her eyes.

The guards are kicking and punching the prisoners as they rush to help their fallen comrade. As the other guards lift her up and carry her away. The acne-pocked guard stays behind. He is kicking Muhammad. He growls: "He violated her! I saw it. He violated her! I'm gonna' kill the bastard. I'm gonna' cut his balls off and hang 'em on the wall!"

The other guards turn on the hoses and spray down the

guard gone crazy as well as the prisoners. The intense water pressure raises then drops, tumbles then shakes everyone in a macabre water ballet, the dancers twitching and turning and flopping about in the cold, cold water in a command performance no one will be able to recall when asked what happened on that dark, or was it a sunny, day.

The Third Memory
Fatimah's Marriage...

And so they were married, Muhammad and the girl named Fatimah, in a ceremony officiated by, and attended only by, Imam Ali.

The three meet at dawn in a dusty palm grove alongside the river near the old iron bridge under a gnarled and ancient olive tree whose branches reach out over the water be- low. Fatimah is, in her heart, shy, numb, uncertain, afraid. But Marium has given Fatimah the wedding cloak she wore when she married Yusuf, and fixed Fatimah's hair with small flowers and lined her eyes with charcoal and dyed her hands with intricate henna patterns so that Fatimah's beauty overshadows her fear. And as Muhammad, following the words of Imam Ali, tries to make his promises to her, he falters and can barely speak when he actually looks into Fatimah's eyes and places a cheap tin ring on her finger. And in that moment, what was lust and guilt and desire turns to love.

That night, Muhammad trembles in anticipation for although he has seen Fatimah naked many times, and in his mind he has been with her, wrapped himself around her, slept next to her, made love to her; in reality, he is a virgin, a bumbling lover with no knowledge or experience in the arts of seduction or sex.

And Fatimah's plight is even more complicated. She has been brutally introduced to the mechanics of copulation, but the passion of lovemaking holds no fascination. The girl is not seeking romance in her wedding bed, only security and protection from a cruel, indifferent world. And so she lies there in the darkness, unmoving, but also silent, unresisting. She allows Muhammad to lift her gown. She allows Muhammad to touch her. She allows Muhammad to enter her. And to her relief, within seconds, he has released himself inside her and it is finished.

In the morning, Fatimah rises early avoiding her new husband's eyes. When he approaches her, she turns away. When he touches her, her body grows rigid.

"You are not happy," he says to her. "I am," she answers.

"I did not please you."

"I am pleased you are my husband"

"Then why will you not look at me?"

"A wife should not be bold. I am humble in your presence."

"It is I who should be humble before you." "I am your servant, Muhammad. I will obey your commands."

"Then I command that you love me," he says.

"Then I will do so," she replies.

But Fatimah soon learns that love is not so easily created, nor are memories so easily erased. She sees Hakim in the marketplace. He is in a crisp, clean uniform. He has grown a mustache. He wears a big, black gun on his right hip. He stands erect, powerful, dominating. When he sees Fatimah, he greets her. She refuses to acknowledge him. He smiles.

Waiting.

Fatimah walks alongside the highway. A police car roars past her, the back draft creates a breeze which presses her abaya against her body. The car screeches to a halt. Hakim opens the door, climbs out of the vehicle and plants himself on the shoulder of the road so that Fatimah must walk around him. She refuses to do so. Instead she goes down on her haunches and covers her face completely as the trucks and busses and cars speed past. He watches her. Waiting.

Fatimah walks with Marium to the bathhouse. As they turn the corner and enter through the arched doorway on the women's side, Hakim is leaving from the men's side. When he sees her, he turns and reenters the bathhouse. As she lets the hot water from a tin pail wash over her body and she tries to feel clean, she cannot because she knows somehow he is watching. And waiting.

Fatimah does not tell Muhammad that Hakim is waiting. She only becomes more unavailable to Muhammad as she hurries through the day cleaning and washing and cooking and washing and cleaning yet again. And she seldom speaks to Muhammad. And when she does, she is curt, abrupt, cold.

Muhammad tries to find work, but work is not so easily found for a man who knows everything in The Book, but nothing of money, computers, driving, mechanics, cooking or any other job-related activity. Eventually he finds work sorting through mounds of garbage and extracting anything of value.

When he returns home at night, he smells, a help for Fatimah because she then has a reason to avoid him. After a bowl of thin soup, he studies The Book while she sews clothes for people with money, and with each pass of thread and needle, she makes more money than Muhammad makes in a week.

One spring morning early, when the birds are singing, Fatimah brings her night's work to a small gated house on the edge of the town. A maid answers the door and ushers Fatimah into the main room. She leaves, Then Hakim enters. Fatimah's skin tingles. Heat races through her body.

Hakim approaches her. "Do not be afraid." She turns away from him, and despises herself for the desire she is feeling inside.

Hakim stops and does not touch her. He bows. "I am sorry for what happened that morning. We were young men… out of control. We did a terrible thing."

Fatimah is trembling. Her eyes averted.

He touches the side of her face and turns her gaze toward him. He stares into her eyes.

"Ever since…"

Fatimah begins to cry. Tears roll down her cheeks.

"Please…" he says.

Fatimah's tears flow even more freely. She is sobbing, gasping for breath. Her body is wracked with uncontrollable spasms.

Hakim wraps his arms around her and holds her against his chest until she finally runs out of tears and there is no more pain to release.

"Fatimah…"

Fatimah looks up.

Hakim again touches her cheek, and this time places a kiss upon her lips, then another, then another as he nibbles her soft lower lip. The heat rises up again inside Fatimah. She does not resist. In fact she grows hungry, aggressive. She arches her back and draws his kisses to her neck, her breasts.

She purrs with desire.

And then he is on her, all over her, inside her. His thrusts are deep and penetrating. Her response rhythmic, powerful. And in that moment, they are one together before they collapse entwined on the soft scarlet carpet. And as her pleasure recedes, Fatimah grows ever more rigid and withdrawn as inside her head the words hammer on the anvil of her brain: betrayal, betrayal.

Meanwhile, Muhammad is sifting through a particularly slimy mound of garbage when he spies a glint of yellow metal. Slowly, carefully, he cleans the grime and grit and sludge from the metal and discovers he has found a gold wedding ring! He quickly, quietly slips the ring into his pocket and goes back to work cleaning a coil of copper wire.

That evening, Muhammad returns home with his prize only to find his house dark and silent. No dinner awaits him. No cleaning is taking place. Fatimah is lying on their small bed blankly staring at the wall.

Muhammad sits on the bed next to her. "Peace be with you."

Fatimah does not answer.

"Are you feeling sick, Fatimah?" Still no answer.

"I have a surprise for you."

Fatimah blinks and turns toward Muhammad, for the first time acknowledging his presence, but his odor causes her to squint and sniff.

"I know I have not yet washed, but I was worried about you when I came home. Here. Look. I want you to see this."

Excited, he pulls out the ring. "I want you to have it."

He takes her hand, removes the tin ring he cave her on their wedding day and places the gold ring on her finger. It is a perfect fit.

Muhammad smiles. "I am so happy." He kisses her. "I love you."

Fatimah continues to stare at the wall. Muhammad leaves to clean up.

Fatimah looks down at her finger. She studies the ring as if it were a curiosity. Then she gets up and lights the stove to prepare dinner for her husband.

Days pass. Fatimah does not see Hakim again, and he does not stalk here. She keeps her secret close to her heart and throws a mask across her face as she struggles through each moment, each hour.

Muhammad continues to work long hours and to read from The Book late into the night. He does not approach his beautiful young wife. He does not press her for love. He withdraws ever more deeply inside himself.

One day as he heads for the garbage dump, Muhammad runs into Imam Ali.

"I have not seen you at prayers," says Ali.

"I have been praying at home," says Muhammad.

Imam Ali studies Muhammad. "What is wrong, my son?"

"Nothing is wrong. I am tired."

"I think there is more."

"No. I need to go."

"Let me walk beside you, Muhammad," and Imam Ali slows his pace to match Muhammad's.

"Ahmed came to see me yesterday. You remember him. My only student more pious than you? Well, he is having trouble at home. He asked me, 'Why would God allow trouble to enter my marriage? Did he not bless our union?'

"Well, I answered, not everything made in heaven is easy

and beautiful. It is true that your marriage was blessed by God and made in heaven. But then again, so are thunder and lightning."

Imam Ali laughs, but Muhammad remains silent.

"I warned you it would not be easy, Muhammad. She is a very troubled young girl. She will always be a troubled young girl after…after what happened to her."

Muhammad interrupts. "There is nothing wrong with her. She is a good wife. She cares for me."

"Then why are you in pain, Muhammad?"

"I am the problem. I am the failure. She is young and beautiful. I have nothing to offer her. I work in a garbage dump."

"You have much to offer. You should finish your studies. You should preach The Word. You should teach The Word."

"Leave me alone, Imam Ali."

"I will. For now. Peace be with you. Muhammad."

"And with you," Muhammad mumbles.

That night Muhammad arrives home to find his wife smiling. She throws her arms around him and greets him with a kiss. He is pleased, but also wary. What has changed?

"I am different now, my husband." Fatimah announces to Muhammad,

"I can see that. But what has changed?"

"I am with child."

Muhammad grins, reaches out, takes her in his arms and holds tightly to her. Then his body tightens. He pulls away. "But…?"

"That first night. Our first night," she lies. "I wanted to be sure before I told you."

Muhammad hugs her again. "I will be a worthy father. I

will leave the garbage dump. I will become a man of God. I will be…"

Fatimah puts a finger to his lips. "Shhh…just be here for us. That is enough."

But it is not enough for Muhammad. He does leave the dump and he returns to Imam Ali and continues his studies. The imam gives him a small stipend to teach a few classes so that Imam Ali can be free to minister to the elderly and the sick during the day.

When he is home, Muhammad no longer reads all night. Instead he arranges his life around Fatimah.

Fatimah decides she will not see Hakim anymore and to hide her condition from him if they should meet on the street.

But Hakim is preoccupied with other concerns. Dark clouds of war are gathering over the mountains to the north of the country. Already foreign troops have landed in rebel towns. Foreign ships are gathering off the southern coast, their missiles pointed inland. Soon foreign planes will fill the skies releasing thunder and fire on towns and villages. Death is coming.

But when he realizes Fatimah is not going to come to him, Hakim seeks her out. Finally he spots her buying onions at a small stall on the fringes of the marketplace. She does her best to slip away, but he cuts her off.

"I cannot see you anymore," she whispers.

"You must. I have to go away. I may never see you again."

"That is at it should be."

"War is coming. There will be an invasion."

"They will not come here."

"They will go everywhere. They will be everywhere."

Fatimah considers this. "If what you say is true, then what difference does it make where we go? There will be no place to hide."

"We cannot stop them. Those of us who will fight for our country must fade into the background. Our time will come later."

"I cannot see you, Hakim. I cannot be with you now."

"Something has changed. I can feel it."

"Yes."

"Muhammad?"

"He is trying."

"And you?"

"I am happy."

Hakim is frustrated he grabs her arm. This draws the attention of others, but they only see a policeman questioning a young girl.

"You must see me!"

"You will force me? You will rape me again, Hakim?"

Her words cut through his anger. He lets go of her.

"No. I am sorry. No."

"Then leave me alone. Fight your war."

"Yes, you are right."

He turns to leave her.

"Hakim…"

He turns and focuses on her deep brown eyes. One small tear forms and slides down her cheek.

"May God watch over you."

"I will survive, God willing."

"Peace be with you."

"And with you."

That evening, Fatimah questions Muhammad.

"There is talk of war, Muhammad."

"With the infidels. Yes. The schoolboys talk about it. They are excited."

"You will not fight."

"I am a man of God."

"Some say this is a war over God. A holy war."

"Imam Ali says it is a war about oil. He says clerics and believers should pray and not take up arms. Let the infidels and nonbelievers do each other in."

"What should we do?"

"Nothing."

Fatimah places her hand on her lower abdomen.

"The baby..."

"...will be born in peace and love. A child of God."

"Yes. That will be good."

They wrap their arms around each other. They kiss. For the moment, all is calm and all is bright. Faith is strong. Love dominates. And their hope springs eternal.

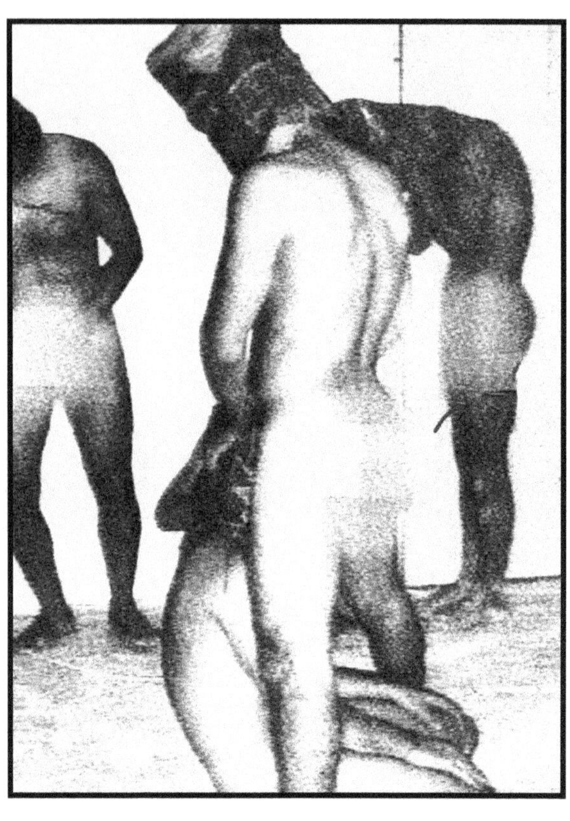

The Fourth Day
A Circle of Friends...

I am back in my…in my what? I guess it's a prison cell. I am naked, but the sack is again over my head. I cannot see but know I am not alone.

They are watching me. But I am so very still, quiet, barely, barely breathing. I am a dried-up baked-in-the-sun worm, not a wiggly worm. I am boring. Useless. Maybe they will go away.

But the group standing over Muhammad does not go away. The acne-pocked reaches down and roughly turns Muhammad over onto his back. It is not a pretty sight. There are open wounds, running, pustulating sours. Even The Captain turns away. He speaks to another man—slight, intense, shaved head but full, flowing beard. Light olive skin and dark, black hooded eyes. "Ask him his name."

A voice speaks to me in words I understand. "What is your name?"

I do not answer. He smacks my head. I understand where this is going. I will speak.

"Muhammad. Muhammad Shakir." I am startled by the hoarse, raspy croak that escapes my lips.

"What was your unit?"

"My unit?"

"What group were you fighting with?"

"I am not a fighter. I am a man of God."

"Do men of God kill people?"

"I have not killed anyone."

"Do you know why you're here?" "No, I do not."

Someone whacks the back of my head through the sack.

"I swear by all that is holy, I do not know why I am here."

The Interrogator turns from the prisoner to The Captain. "He doesn't remember any- thing."

"Tell him we will kill him if he doesn't tell us what we know he knows."

"Muhammad…we will kill you if you don't tell us what you know."

"'Every soul must taste of death,' praise God."

"He wants to die."

"He's the one who screamed, "God is great, and broke up the pyramid, isn't he?"

"Yes, sir. He is the one."

"So…His God against our God."

"Your God, sir."

"Yes, of course, you're…I see."

"No problem, sir. No offense taken."

Yes, well…anyway, this one will talk, I promise you that. He will tell us every single little detail…he will give up all of his friends…he will betray his family…and then he will burn in a decent Christian hell for all fuckin' eternity."

"Do you want me to tell him that?"

"No. He already knows it. He knows he is among the damned. Let him find out the hard way what happens to those who rise against us, our nation and our God!"

The captain leaves. The Interrogator kneels down next to Muhammad and whispers near his ear.

"You should tell them what the y want to know."

Muhammad does not speak.

"Why not? They know everything anyway."

"Then they know more than I do, I know nothing. I am a simple man of God. There must be some mistake."

"Exactly! My point, exactly, Shakir. You're a good guy — in fact, a Man of God good guy. This whole thing's a mistake. Tell them what they want to hear, and you can go home…a free man. Hell, they don't care. They just want to get the bad guys… not the good guys…like you Muhammad. You're one of the good guy aren't you?"

"Yes, that is true. I am a good guy."

"And you have a wife and kids, right?"

"I have a wife."

"No kids?"

"No."

"Oh, I'm sorry to hear that, Muhammad."

The Interrogator waits.

"So, not man enough to make a baby, huh?"

"It is not because of me."

"Oh, yeah. I'm sure that's the case. It's never the man's fault, is it?"

"I do not know about those things."

"Then how do you know it's not your fault?"

Another long pause.

"I'll bet your wife thinks it's your fault."

"My wife is a good woman. She does not think about these things either."

"So, in fact, we don't know whose fault it is that she was never

able to have a baby, do we now, Muhammad?"

"It is God's will, praise God."

"Hmmm, maybe we can run some tests here, Muhammad, you know, to find out why you can't make babies. We can help you."

"I do not need help."

"That's where you're wrong, Muhammad. We all need help. Every damn one of us in this godforsaken place. We all need help."

The Interrogator pulls out his mobile phone. He mumbles something into his handset. Then he turns back toward Muhammad.

"Help is on the way, bro. Help is on the way."

Within minutes, three guards enter Muhammad's cell. They lift Muhammad off the floor, and carry him down the hallway. The Interrogator walks alongside Muhammad.

"Hey, you know, Muhammad, you hadjis are pretty macho guys. Maybe you can't make a baby because you like men, Muhammad, have you ever thought about that?"

Muhammad doesn't respond.

"I mean, I was watching you on that pyramid. You looked a little excited to me. Little bit of the old chocolate highway intrigues you, Muhammad?"

His head bowed, Muhammad stays focused on the floor, studying the patterns of the lines and the cracks, the stains, the different textures.

"Well, this test may tell us something. Lets hope so, right, Muhammad?"

The small group joins up with a bigger group in the game room, the same room where the pyramid building took place. Again, there are other naked, hooded prisoners and various guards in the room.

The captain speaks: "Today is a therapy session, boys and girls. We've gathered together these totally fucked-up wackos who show signs of psychological disorders and we, as part of our responsibility to these deviants, we will help them use their time with us in a constructive manner."

"Ooooha! Oooooha!"

"So…let's make two rows..."

The guards split the prisoner group into two groups. They position one group standing in front of the other group which they force down onto their knees. It is no accident that the faces of the kneeling group are roughly at the same level as the cocks of the other group.

"Yes…that's perfect…perfect. Guards remove their hoods, now,"

When Muhammad's hood is removed, he finds himself on his knees in front of the same man who was next to him in the pyramid. The man looks at Muhammad, then turns away sickened by the blister's and scabs on Muhammad's face.

Behind him Muhammad's interrogator taunts Muhammad.

"I arranged to have you take this test with your friend, Muhammad."

Muhammad lowers his head.

"But he doesn't seem as attracted to you as you are to him."

The captain is speaking: "Alright, interrogators, explain to your deviant that they are to begin masturbating at my command."

"Ooooha!"

"Those on their knees are to look up at those standing. Those standing will look down at those on their knees."

Muhammad's interrogator explains the situation to Muhammad.

"...and you must stroke your own cock and stare up at the man in front of you until he comes all over your face."

"I will not do this."

"Yes you will."

"Why...why will I do this?"

"Because I am telling you to."

"And why should I obey you?"

"Because you want to stay alive."

"'Every soul must taste of death,' praise God."

"Don't quote that hadji shit to me, Muhammad. If you wanted to die, you would have done so when you were supposed to. So...start playing with yourself, Muhammad, or I'll blow your fuckin' brains out.

The Interrogator takes out his pistol and puts the barrel flush against Muhammad's head. And so Muhammad touches himself although he remains flaccid.

The man standing over Muhammad has fewer inhibitions. In fact, his ministrations have produced an erection of considerable length and girth, and Muhammad finds himself confronting the one-eyed monster no more than a few centimeters distant.

He can also feel the pistol pressed into the back of his neck.

And he can hear The Interrogator whispering in his ear.

"Come on, Muhammad, come on...come on...pretend you're making a baby...huh... come on...that's right...come on now... you don't wanna' die..."

But Muhammad can get no closer to the little death, and in his failure he grows even more afraid because his interrogator is correct...he does not want to die the big death, the real death, and so he tries, stroking harder, faster but his cock remains unchanged.

And then…

The corporal appears with her camera. She wanders slowly around the game room, taking pictures of the many performances taking place. She seems particularly interested in photographing an older man with a salt and pepper beard kneeling before a young, clean shaven man, a boy really, who clearly views the older man with enthusiastic admiration.

Muhammad sees her. He watches her and feels the onset of desire. She finishes with the two she's been photographing, and approaches Muhammad.

Look at me…please look at me…"

The corporal sees the wounded man with the peeling face who dared to kiss her lips.

Ah, yes, I see her eyes flicker… she knows it is me, and I feel…and I feel…and I…

His stroking increases in intensity. He breathing is deeper. The veins in his neck pulsate. His jaw tenses…

The corporal points her camera at Muhammad. He feels his entire body stiffen. He hears the man standing over him begins to moan, begin to groan. The man shouts: "God is great!" And Muhammad feels the man's warm cum on his face.

The corporal is smiling as she captures that picture, then another, and another, and The Interrogator is urging Muhammad on and the room is spinning and he watches The Corporal and he dreams of Fatimah and he feels his seed rising and flowing and then the convulsion, the spasms, crossing over, the darkness complete and total.

When Muhammad awakens he is lying on the floor. He

tries to look and see where he is. His head is covered.

His interrogator speaks.

"Yes, I'm here, Muhammad."

Muhammad lets his body slump back down.

"Well, now we know why you can't make babies, don't we?"

Muhammad assumes his sun-baked, dead worm pose.

"The great Muhammad Shakir…a fuckin' faggot."

"I am not listening. I am not hearing. I am not here. This is not my life. I am not listening…"

But he was.

"And we've got pictures."

The Interrogator laughs.

"Pictures of Muhammad Shakir and his uh…'friend.'"

He laughs again. Then he waits.

"Of course..."

Another long pause.

"Of course, no one really needs to see those pictures."

Muhammad does his best not to react to his interrogator's suggestion, but he is thinking.

The pictures could go away…How do I make the pictures go away…

The Interrogator continues.

"All you have to do is tell us who you were working with… where are they…what are their plans…then, poof! the pictures disappear… that's all it takes…"

Muhammad struggles, not because he is reluctant to give them what they want, but because he does not know the information they desire. He wonders, should he just say nothing? Should he beg them to believe him? Should he make things up?

"It's so easy, Muhammad Shakir…it's so easy just to talk to

us…"

"I cannot…I…I don't know…I am a man of God…I am not a warrior…"

The Interrogator is angry.

"We are not stupid, Muhammad. And we will not be treated as fools…"

He gets up to leave, and as he does so, he aims one last viscous kick at the filthy mess quivering on the floor.

"Aaaagh!"

"Think about talking, Muhammad…"

The Interrogator leaves.

Muhammad drifts away toward sleep. Suddenly he's wide awake!

That screaming has started up again. I can't stand it. Stop screaming! I can't stand it.

The Fourth Memory
The New Imam...

On the very day that Fatimah makes her first visit to the women's clinic where they assure her that she and the new life beginning within her are fit and healthy, bombs start falling from the sky and missiles are launched from distant warships. The country is at war and many other lives will be ending before the day is finished.

Black clouds so thick they block out the sun rise from fires set in the oil fields, massive tremors shake the foundations of buildings in the capitol as if there were a serious earthquake and the thunder of exploding munitions crackles throughout the night as it will for many sleepless nights to come.

Fatimah is frightened, but the war does not come near the town where she and Muhammad live. They hear planes flying overhead. They feel the ground shake when bombs fall on an airfield near their town. They can smell oil fumes and see black soot collect on everything left exposed to the air. There are rumors. There are stories. But there is no death or destruction in their streets.

In many ways her life is easier. Hakim does disappear. She no longer sees him anywhere. People stop quarreling and arguing over little, insignificant things. No one has money. Most everyone is poor. And Muhammad focuses all his attention on her and the baby growing inside her.

"What shall we name him?" he asks her.

"You know it will be a boy?"

"What will we name the baby?"

"You would not want a girl?"

"I would hope, God willing, for a child who will live in service to God."

"Like his father."

"And his grandfather."

"A woman's life does not serve God?"

"A woman's life serves the things of this earth. A woman is of the earth. A man is of the sky."

"Evil things are flying from the sky, Muhammad."

"But they are not God's will."

"How do we know God's will?"

"We cannot, Fatimah. Enough. What shall we name the baby?"

She smiles. "The baby boy.

"Yes."

"It is too early. It would be bad. We should wait. A name will come to us."

When Muhammad tells Imam Ali that Fatimah is pregnant, Imam Ali does not express joy or congratulate Muhammad as Muhammad expects him to. The imam's face is drawn, taught. His eyes are sunken surrounded by deep shadows. He offers no funny stories. It is not even clear that he hears Muhammad's news.

"A great war is coming," says the imam.

"Yes, but it will not come here, to our town,

God willing."

He prods the imam again. "Did you hear me? Fatimah will have our baby?"

"The war will be everywhere. It is a war for souls. We are in the last days."

Muhammad considers the imam's words. "Well, it is written that, 'Whenever they kindle a fire for war God puts it out; they strive to make mischief in the land, and God does not love the mischief-makers.'"

"This will be a war *over* God, Muhammad, and 'The punishment of those who wage war against God and His apostle and strive to make trouble in the land is only this, that they should be murdered or crucified or their hands and their feet should be cut off on opposite sides or they should be imprisoned…' This will be such a holy war, and there will be much suffering and pain and death."

"As it should be when foreigners attack us."

"Perhaps. Perhaps. But I am an imam of joy and happiness. God desires we love, not hate. I do not want war. I am happy you and Fatimah will have a child. I hope there will be a world for the child to live in."

"I have never see you sad. You frighten, Imam Ali."

"I am close to despair, Muhammad."

"'Do not despair of the mercy of God…'"

"I do not despair God's mercy. I despair man's mercy to his fellow man. Already the young men of our school talk of nothing but killing. Already the older boys stop coming to class and disappear. Soon foreign soldiers will be in the streets of our town, in our markets, in our homes. They will even violate the mosques…"

"Then we shall defeat them."

"They have mighty weapons, Muhammad."

"But we have faith."

"Yes, yes. You know, Muhammad, a group of philosophers contemplated for many years, the end of the world. But try as they might, they could not state a time for its coming. Finally they turned to an old beggar and asked him:'Do you know when the end of the world will be?'

'Of course,' said the beggar , 'when I die, that will be the end of the world.'

'When you die? Are you sure?'

'It will be for me at least,' said the beggar.'"

Muhammad is glad to hear a story from his beloved imam, but he is shaken. The message of the story is clear. Muhammad is worried about the profound change in Imam Ali's state of mind.

Then, two days later, the first missile strikes the town square on market day.

Fatimah is in the market. She hears, like all the others, the sound of an approaching aircraft. She, like the others, ignores the sound thinking it's the noise of a harmless plane.

The explosion knocks her off her feet. She is thrown violently to the ground and ends up underneath a vegetable cart as the debris rains down around her. She sees onions and beets and wheat and rice strewn across the ground in front of her. There's a tomato, squashed, and another smashed against a splintered railing. She looks more closely. She shivers. Are those red objects really tomatoes or…?

She tries to move but she is pinned beneath loose timbers. Panicked, she searches for a way to escape. She studies the timbers. She sees that the rubble on top of her must have been from the butcher's stall. There are freshly cut slabs of meat scattered about—shank, stomach, brisket, arms, hands… Wait. Arms…hands! The horror hits her. She struggles to maintain consciousness. Then she looses strength and passes out.

Muhammad hears the explosion. At first he is confused. Then he sees the crowds running toward the market. He sees smoke. He sees fire. He hears screaming. He runs faster.

He arrives in the midst of total chaos. Men are carrying bleeding and moaning wounded bodies. Women are screaming and tearing at their garments. Little children wander about with dazed expressions on their faces. A mangy old dog limps and howls and struggles to stay on her feet.

Muhammad opens his mouth and tries to call out to Fatimah, but no words escape his lips. He clears his throat and tries again, "Fatimah!"

There is no answer.

He calls out again, "Fatimah?" He listens. Nothing.

Muhammad is dizzy. The palms of his hands are moist. His legs wobble. He staggers forward screaming, "Fatimah! Fatimah! Fatimah!"

A woman he barely recognizes beneath the dust on her face and the blood smeared across her forehead, grabs Muhammad's arm. "She is over there." The woman points toward a pile of broken wood and torn canvas. "I saw her. On the ground."

Muhammad pushed forward through the crowd. He sees his wife collapsed on the ground. He cries out, "Fatimah!" When she does not respond, he weeps and falls to his knees next to her. He grabs her hand and presses it to his lips. He whispers, "Fatimah?"

She opens her eyes. "Fatimah!"

"The baby?"

Muhammad leaps to his feet, adrenaline flowing, he lifts the broken timbers and other debris away from Fatimah. Then he returns to his knees and leans over her.

"The baby?" She asks again.

Muhammad ignores her question. He asks, "Are you hurt?"

"The baby?" She repeats.

Muhammad gathers Fatimah in his arms and stands. He frantically searches the area, trying to get his bearings. He follows the others carrying their wounded to the hospital three blocks away.

The situation at the hospital is nearly as a chaotic as it was in the marketplace. The tile floors are slippery with blood. Patients and doctors and nurses are all talking at once and in the resulting babble, little is understood. And more casualties arrive all the time.

Muhammad sits on the floor in a hospital hallway, Fatimah in his arms. He rocks back and forth, mumbling over and over again, "Please help me...please help me."

Finally, a young doctor whose white coat is streaked with red blood, black ashes and bits of flesh, takes pity on the bearded man rocking the wounded young woman and begging for attention.

"Peace be with you," he says as he leans over Muhammad.

"And with you," says Muhammad. "Your daughter?"

"My wife. She was in the marketplace."

The doctor checks for a pulse. He gets one. It's strong. There is hope.

"Do you know if she is injured?"

"She was under...under a collapsed stall. I do not know how badly she was hurt."

The doctor notices blood on her robe near her waist. "She is bleeding…"

"No…no…" Muhammad mumbles.

"…but her pulse is very strong."

Muhammad grabs at hope.

The doctor says, "She is young and strong. She will live, God willing. Certainly, it is worth the effort." He looks around. "Come. Bring her in here." He indicates a small room behind them. "I will examine her."

The doctor opens the door into a small room where the beds are already filled with six other wounded. Muhammad follows with Fatimah. The doctor indicates he should put her on the floor.

"Undo her robes."

Muhammad is shocked. "Here…now?"

"Yes. If you want me to care or her. We have no time for modesty. Do it."

Muhammad undresses Fatimah. He sees one of the other casualties, a young man with a bandage around his head, turn and leer over the body of the naked young woman.

"Please…" says Muhammad.

The young man turns his face to the wall. The doctor moves quickly. He examines her limbs, presses his fingers against her belly, her chest, over her heart. He listens through his stethoscope.

Fatimah stirs. She opens her eyes. She blinks. She looks around. She sees the young doctor touching her. She frowns.

"We are in a hospital," says Muhammad. "You were injured. In the explosion. In the market."

"Yes." Then she closes her eyes again.

The doctor is finished. He looks toward Muhammad.

"You may cover her now."

The young man on the bed turns to catch one last glimpse.

Muhammad yells, "Have you no decency?"

"Shhh. Be merciful," whispers the doctor, "he may not live the night."

Muhammad continues to dress Fatimah.

The doctor rises onto one knee. "I can find nothing wrong with her…"

Muhammad sighs.

"…except…"

"Yes?"

"I'm sorry. Was she pregnant?"

"Was?"

"She has miscarried."

"Miscarried?"

"She has lost the child."

A plaintive wail escapes Muhammad.

"I am sorry," says the doctor, "but you are very lucky. She is healthy. Unharmed. You can have other children. I must go. You may take her home. She will be fine, God willing."

Muhammad is stunned. He carries Fatimah through the streets where sirens still scream, black smoke rises into the sky and the evening call to prayer wails in the background.

Later, Muhammad kneels next to their bed while Fatimah sleeps fitfully. Suddenly she bolts upright and cries out. Muhammad, startled, takes her hand and caresses her arm. She lays back on the bed. "The baby?"

"Sleep," says Muhammad.

"I do not have a baby, do I?"

"No, my love. You do not."

Fatimah does not cry. She shows no emotion at all.

Muhammad reaches out to her, but she pushes his arm away.

"Fatimah, please…"

But Fatimah does not speak.

Early the next morning, even before the early light of dawn appears, Muhammad goes to the mosque to speak with Imam Ali. The imam is prostrate on his rug praying fervently. Muhammad waits until he rises.

"Peace be with…"

"…And upon all of us in these times."

"Fatimah was injured in the market."

"She is alive?"

"Yes."

"You are fortunate. We will have many funeral processions through the streets today."

"She is no longer with child."

"That is unfortunate. You can have another, God willing."

"She will not talk."

"This too will pass."

"I am not certain."

"Then, we shall see. But I have other duties to attend to. Will you help me today, Muhammad Shakir?"

"Yes…let us do God's work."

After morning prayers, the bodies begin to appear, brought by family and friends, wrapped in white, laid out on pallets to be carried by the pallbearers to the cemetery on the edge of town.

There are sixteen, seven children, five women, four men when Imam Ali and Muhammad Shakir read the prayers for the dead. Then the pallets are lifted onto the shoulders of the grieving. Their are laments and much ululating from old women completely draped in black from head to toe.

After the funeral cortege has proceeded for a few blocks, they are joined by a band of men in black wearing ski masks and carrying automatic weapons. The men walk silently alongside the bodies until the procession reaches the cemetery. Then, as the bodies are lowered into the hard dusty ground, and more prayers are said, and more cries erupt from the crowd, the men fire their weapons into the air.

The firing ignites the mourners to even greater frenzy. The men fire another volley. Imam Ali walks toward the armed men with his hand raised in the air.

"Stop!"

The masked men continue to fire.

"I said, stop! There has been enough violence."

One of the men steps forward. "We are done with weak lamentations. We are done with suffering. We will avenge the deaths of our mothers and fathers, our brothers and sisters, our children!"

"You will do what you will," says Imam Ali, "but do not fire another shot here."

"By whose order," asks the masked man. "By mine," says Imam Ali.

The man pulls a pistol from his waistband and places it against the imam's head. "Then I cancel that order," he says as he fires a bullet into Imam Ali's brain. The cleric crumbles to the ground. The men in black fire volley after volley into the air. The older men and women disperse into the shadows, but the young boys and young men dance and chant for death to the foreign invaders as Muhammad, for the second time in two days, cradles a loved one in his lap and weeps.

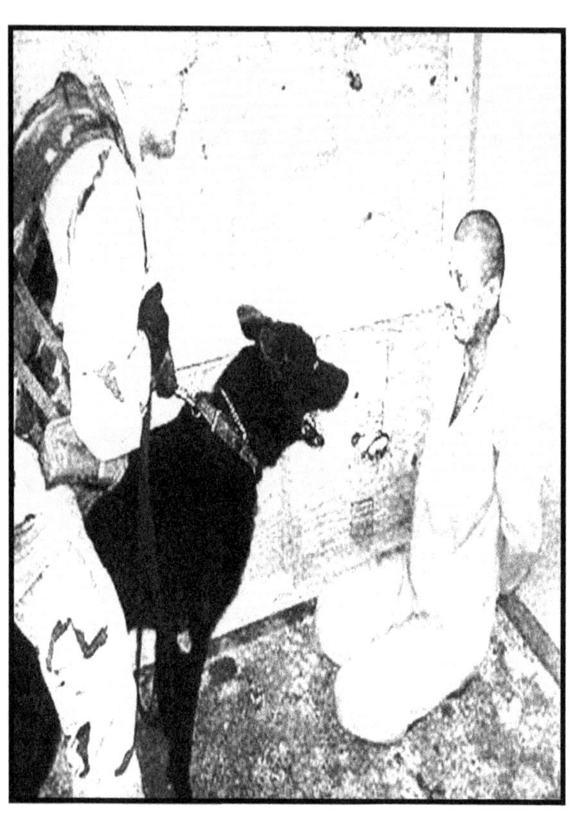

The Fifth Day
Going to the Dogs...

A waning crescent moon fades and dawn sweeps across the desert as a long and haunting canine keening reverberates through the corridors of Muhammad's cell block. That lonely howl drowns out the bugle's ring, the orders shouted, the marching boots, the muezzin's call. It drowns out the screaming. Muhammad, hearing that ancient sound, stirs, near waking but not yet conscious, the hairs on the back of his neck rise, his spine tingles and the fear spreads within his soul triggered by the call of the wolf.

Muhammad opens his eyes, but the covering is still in place. Yet he senses…he knows he is not alone.

It is The Interrogator.

"She lost one of her puppies last night. She's sad. And angry."

"It is not easy to lose a child."

"How would you know?"

Muhammad's hood shakes back and forth.

"Oh, well, whatever…isn't the man of God going to say his morning prayers?"

"I cannot pray properly tied up like this…an animal ready for slaughter."

The Interrogator brings out a knife and slices Muhammad's bonds.

"Aaagh!"

Muhammad's body finds no comfort in release. But he can move.

"I will pray. Which way the south?"

"Hmmm. Interesting question."

"Please."

The Interrogator points.

"That way."

"But I cannot see you."

"That's true. You can't."

"Then how am I to know."

"I could remove your hood."

"Yes."

"But I need something."

"Yes."

"Talk to me."

"Yes."

"Alright then."

The Interrogator removes Muhammad's hood and does his best to suppress the urge to vomit when he sees the scabs. Instead, he points south again.

Muhammad bows three times in that direction and murmurs. "…no God but God…God is great. All praise is due Him, Who created the heavens and the earth and made the day and the night. Through Him, and in Him and with Him, I am… and without Him, I am not. God is my salvation, and if God wills it, He will bring me out of this darkness into His Light. Praise God. "

Muhammad remains on his knees, his forehead on the

cool concrete, not moving , breathing deeply, at peace.

The Interrogator allows Muhammad a few minutes.

"Who is your leader?"

"God."

"I thought we were going to talk?"

Muhammad is frightened.

"I am talking."

"Yes, but you are not telling me anything."

"I do not know anything."

The Interrogator reaches down and picks up a file folder. He opens it and reads.

"Your name is Muhammad Shakir?"

"Yes…I think so."

"And you are the imam of your community mosque?"

"I am?"

"We're not getting anywhere, Muhammad."

"But I do not know where to go."

"The truth shall set you free."

"Truth requires knowing."

"You know your name."

"Yes."

"You know you have a wife…"

"Yes."

"You know you have no children."

"Yes."

"You know you preach against us."

"No."

"You know you send young men to kill us."

"No."

"You know you are yourself a murderer!"

"No."

The Interrogator throws the file on the floor. Angry, he pulls out his cell phone and makes a call. Then he takes a deep breath.

"It was sad how she lost her puppy."

Muhammad is silent.

"One of you vermin took it from her and ate it. She hates vermin."

Muhammad can hear the snarling and growling, the slap of boots on concrete, chains, sharply worded commands. He crawls to the corner of his cell, and tucks his head between his legs, his arms wrapped around the back of his neck. He refuses to look when the animal enters his cell.

The animal is a half German Shepherd, half wolf female dog, over two-and-one-half feet tall measured from her shoulders and 137 pounds of tightly wound muscle. Her lips are pulled back from her gums revealing sharp, white incisors and massive cuspids. A formidable, powerful girl barely kept under control by two guards each of which tugs on a restraint.

The Interrogator is laughing.

"Ha!...Muhammad meet Schatzi.

Muhammad refuses to look.

"Schatzi, meet Muhammad."

Schatzi lunges toward Muhammad still cowering in the corner.

Two more guards enter the cell. They grab Muhammad's arms and pull them out to the side. Muhammad is forced to look at the animal. He promptly pees on the floor. The Interrogator laughs.

"An appropriate response, Muhammad."

To the guards: "Release her." They remove the restraints

from around the dog's neck. The dog slowly approaches Muhammad, her head down between her shoulders, ready to attack.

"Here, Schatzi!"

The dog immediately relaxes and ambles over to The Interrogator's side.

"Sit!"

The dog sits calmly next to The Interrogator, but she keeps an eye on Muhammad.

"Down."

Schatzi lies down next to The Interrogator. The Interrogator reaches into his pocket and gives the dog a treat, She gulps it quickly and then rests her head on her front paws. Placid and gentle as a lamb.

"You will notice, Muhammad, that Schatzi obeys me immediately, unquestionably. In return she is well cared for and she gets a treat."

Muhammad is too terrified to respond.

"Schatzi understands how things work around here."

Muhammad nods.

"Speak!"

Schatzi growls.

"Now, you talk."

Muhammad is thinking of the story he wants to tell The Interrogator.

The Interrogator is angry.

"Talk!"

He stands up. Schatzi leaps to her feet.

"Talk!"

Schatzi moves forward. She stands inches away from Muhammad's cock growling ferociously, her teeth completely bared.

Suddenly, without warning, the guards holding onto Muhammad's arms let go, and the dog attacks. Muhammad twists his body and the bite hits his left buttock rather than his cock. There is torn flesh and deep puncture marks at the point of the wound, Blood drips down Muhammad's leg.

"Aaagh!"

"Schatzi, sit!"

"Sorry about that. But you don't have to worry."

He strokes the dogs neck.

"She's had all her shots. She has no disease."

He kneels down next to her and checks her mouth.

"Did you know, Muhammad, that a dog's mouth is cleaner than a human mouth? Less bacteria. You probably won't even get an infection."

To the dog, "Good, girl."

"What is the difference if I receive one more wound?"

"Ah, you can talk."

"Yes."

"So...what do you have to say?"

"I am guilty."

"Of...?"

"Of what you say I am guilty of. I will sign a confession that I am guilty."

"That's good. That's a start."

"A start? What else do you want from me?"

"Information, Muhammad. Names. Places. Dates. Organizational structure. Targets. Methods. Should I go on?"

"I am not of that world. I do not know these things."

"So, we're right back at the beginning. This is the way you want it?"

"My answer has nothing to do with what I want or do not want. My answer is the truth, as God is my witness, I do not know these things."

The Interrogator exhales deeply. He grabs a restraint from one of the guards and places it around the dog's neck. He holds on with both hands,

"Schatzi…attack!"

The dog leaps toward Muhammad growling and barking and snarling, her hips coiled, her shoulders back, her neck straining forward. She would rip Muhammad apart except The Interrogator keeps her just inches short of Muhammad's body.

I am lost except for my faith in God, and the Book…Ah! yes, wherein the Prophet writes: '…there is no animal on earth but that God is the sustenance of it…' Yes. So…I must draw my strength to face this animal from God.

Muhammad closes his eyes. He opens his heart to God's protection and lets go of all his fear.

It is also written in the parable of the dog, that "…if you attack him he lolls out his tongue…" So, I shall attack!

Muhammad gathers up all his strength. He raises his arms in the air, turns his hands into giant claws, his face, already frightening, into a mask of rage, his chest expanded, he is a terrifying specter.

"AAAaaaaagh!"

He moves toward Schatzi!

Amazingly, the dog stops her attack. Muhammad lumbers forward again like an angry bear walking on it's hind legs.

"AAAaaaaagh!"

Schatzi whimpers. She lies down on her back, completely submissive before this terrible creature who's assaulting her.

The Interrogator is screaming. "Up! Attack!"

Schatzi looks at him. Then she looks up at Muhammad bear. She stays on her back.

The Interrogator kicks the dog, who then growls at *him*. Muhammad sees the reaction, and before anyone can stop him, he turns his fury onto The Interrogator. As Muhammad attacks, the dog also leaps at The Interrogator who is knocked onto the concrete beneath both Muhammad and Schatzi. This time it is The Interrogator who is screaming for help. The remaining guards move in. They put restraints on the dog. Whack Muhammad with their clubs. Pull The Interrogator away from the attack.

The Interrogator is bleeding from his scalp. His uniform is ripped and torn. His left arm hangs loosely at his side. He is bewildered.

He walks over to Muhammad who's being pinned to the floor by one guard while being punched in the kidneys by another.

To the guards. "Stop."

To Muhammad: *"How did you do that?"*

Through a wall of pain, puffy eyes and broken teeth, through blood and mucus Muhammad says: *"The God of the Book, or the God of the hadjis."*

"I know of no God of the hadjis."

The Interrogator turns to the guards holding Schatzi. "Release her."

The guards let go of Schatzi's restraints. She stays calm, then pads over to Muhammad's face and licks his wounds.

"Your God is a powerful God, Muhammad."

"He is not my God, He is God."

"Why does your...why does God want you to kill us?"

"He does not."

"Then why did you kill?"

Muhammad puts his arm around Schatzi's neck and scratches her chest.

"I did not. I am a man of God."

The Interrogator retrieves the file he had thrown on the floor. He holds it out toward Muhammad.

"I have your file. I have pictures."

"This is not a record of my life."

"What I have just seen is extraordinary. So, I will research these records. We shall see."

He signals to the guards. "Go." He commands Schatzi. "Come here."

But Schatzi lies down next to Muhammad and refuses to budge.

That night Muhammad hears no more screaming, and the rats stay safe inside the walls.

The Fifth Memory
Winds of Change...

Days pass after the market bombing and Imam Ali's murder. Fatimah still does not speak. Weeks pass. Fatimah cleans and cooks and cleans beyond any conceivable necessity, but she does not speak.

Muhammad brings her to the hospital. They see the young doctor who cared for her after the bombing. He examines Fatimah. Then he talks to both Fatimah and Muhammad.

"Fatimah, there is nothing wrong with you...physically. You can speak. Do you know that."

Fatimah indicates nothing. She sits with her head bowed apparently studying her hands folded in her lap.

The doctor turns to Muhammad. "She is in shock. The baby. The bombing."

"Yes, but..."

"I don't know what to tell you beyond those facts."

"What can I do?"

"Nothing. Everything. I can't say what will happen. I don't think..." he turns toward Fatimah "...I don't think Fatimah knows what she will do."

Muhammad leaves the doctor's office despondent. More

time passe, and still there is no change.

During this time, Muhammad carries out the duties previously performed by Imam Ali in the mosque and the school. Gradually, the congregation acquires a certain degree of trust in Muhammad, and an elder, Sheik Wahad Majih, visits him in the mosque's courtyard after prayers.

As they sit, a cooling breeze rustles the leaves on the lemon tree and tickles the sheik's long gray beard. A sparrow picking at seeds hops along the ground near the bench where the two men are sitting.

"You are still young," says the sheik.

"And not very wise," Muhammad adds tactfully.

"Wise enough," the sheik responds.

"Thank you." Muhammad bows his head. "God is giving us difficult times in which to live."

"The times are difficult."

"We want a voice to speak for us in the manner and thoughts of Imam Ali, may he enjoy peace in paradise."

"He was my teacher. He was my guide."

The sheik stops, stares at the ground and considers his next words carefully. "We will be asked to fight the foreigners…"

"The men in black are already speaking to the young."

"…And we will be asked to support the foreigners."

"Emissaries have visited me."

"We…we would prefer not to support anyone, but instead, to support God."

"That would also be my thought."

"It is better for commerce. Much is at stake. Our crops. Our shops, Our marketplace."

"And our faith."

"Yes, of course, praise God."

"So…"

"So…"

A very ripe lemon falls from the tree startling the sparrow who flies away. The breeze dies down. Sheik Majih sits patiently, staring off into the mid-distance.

"We have conferred."

"Yes."

"There is the matter of your birth."

"I understand."

"And Yusuf 's death."

"May he also rest peacefully in paradise."

"Still…we have decided."

Muhammad waits. The sheik is still in no hurry. The sparrow returns and picks at more seeds.

"We have decided we want you to be imam of our mosque, to replace Imam Ali."

Muhammad bows toward the sheik. "I accept your decision to be imam, but I cannot replace Imam Ali. He had wisdom and compassion far greater than I could possibly call upon."

"He taught you well. You will grow."

"And I will work very hard, Sheik Majih."

And so Muhammad Shakir becomes imam of the small mosque, in the small town alongside the big river in the dusty farmland of the central valley. On his way home, he stops to visit with his mother, Marium, to tell her the news.

"Yusuf is smiling on us now," says Marium as she kisses her son.

"I also feel his spirit. May he guide me through the difficult tasks ahead."

"He will be there for you."

"And you?"

"I am always with you."

Muhammad hesitates, then he looks directly into his mother's eyes. His own show a few tears.

"Fatimah…"

"She needs time…"

"I need her."

"God willing, she, her mind, will come back to you soon."

"If not?"

"Then that is your burden. Carrying it will be your grace."

Muhammad accepts his mother's kiss. Then he heads home to Fatimah who is once again cleaning the steps where one enters their home.

"Please…come inside." He takes her hand. They sit on the narrow bed facing each other.

"I have been asked to be imam."

There is no reaction from Fatimah. "Are you not happy for me…for us?" Fatimah's eyes are blank.

Muhammad tries to kiss her, but she does not respond and so his lips touch ice.

"We could have another…you can become…"

Fatimah sighs.

"Please, Fatimah, come back to me." Fatimah sits and stares straight ahead.

Muhammad leaves the bed and goes out of the house. He stretches his hands toward the sky in silent supplication. Fatimah returns to sweeping the steps.

The next day, the men in black visit Imam Muhammad Shakir at the mosque. Their apparent leader speaks to Muhammad in a voice Muhammad recognizes.

"It is you, Hakim," says Muhammad.

"I prefer to be called Ashur, our Assyrian ancestor's God of War."

"Then I will call you Ashur. What do you want from me, Ashur?"

"The foreigners are at the capital. Soon they will occupy our entire country."

"A situation to be regretted."

"A situation to be resisted."

"I will not dispute that."

"Resisted by everyone, Muhammad Shakir, Imam Muhammad Shakir. You have influence."

"You exaggerate."

"You have influence. You must preach in favor of resistance."

"I preach in favor of God, praise God."

"God wills us to resist. This is a holy war. God is on our side."

" You should be imam, Hak…, sorry, Ashur…you should be imam, since you speak with God and know his intentions."

"Do not mock me, Muhammad. You have influence but I have power, the power of the man who holds the gun."

"Here is my word: I will not preach against you…"

"Good."

"…But I will not preach in favor of resistance either. There will be too many dead. From reports I hear, there already are."

"We have always fought our oppressors, and freedom from the foreigners has always caused us many deaths. That is the price we must pay."

"Perhaps you are right. I will not disagree. I have suffered greatly from the foreigners."

"How?"

"My wife, Fatimah, was pregnant. She was injured and lost our baby in the market bombing."

This statement causes Hakim to recoil almost as if Muhammad had slapped him in the face.

"Fatimah was…pregnant?"

Muhammad is too wrapped up in his own pain to take in Hakim's reactions. "Yes, and now she will not speak. I hate the foreigners, but I will preach the message of compassion and reconciliation. That is my mission, my duty, to God and my mosque, praise God."

Hakim has lost track of the message he is delivering to Muhammad. His thoughts are on Fatimah…and the odds that her loss was also his loss. He abruptly ends his debate with Muhammad. "I must go now."

"Peace be with you, Hak…Ashur. Peace be with you."

Hakim does not respond in kind. He signals to his men, and they are gone.

Muhammad prostrates himself in prayer. He prays for his country. He prays for his people. He prays for his town. He prays for his mother. He prays for Fatimah. He even says a prayer for Hakim and the men in black who will die fighting the foreigners. And then he prays one last prayer for himself, for the strength and compassion and love to serve God's will.

Later that evening, Muhammad paces back and forth as he tells Fatimah about his meeting with Hakim at the mosque.

"He calls himself The Ashur of Revenge now."

Fatimah is seated so that Muhammad cannot see her face. She appears motionless, but her features are contorted in agony as she tries to maintain control.

"He wants me to preach in favor of the resistance."

Fatimah stands, grabs a broom and begins to sweep

the floor.

"What are you doing? You have already swept three times."

Fatimah continues sweeping.

"I was wrong. The war will be here. What am I saying? The war is here. It has already changed our lives. We will never be the same." Muhammad looks toward Fatimah. She is crying.

Muhammad takes Fatimah into his arms and holds her while she weeps.

"God will protect us," he says quietly. "We have already suffered enough. He cannot ask for more. Not from you and me."

Fatimah is not thinking about God. Fatimah is thinking about Hakim. Hakim is fighting to avenge her! Hakim is fighting for their dead baby! Hakim is a man! She pulls away from Muhammad and vows not only to never speak to him, but never to let him touch her again.

Two days later, the foreigners swarm through the town. They do not look like human beings. They are aliens from another planet, beasts from nightmares, from tales of the battles against devils at the end of the world.

They ride in monstrous vehicles which sprout numerous antennae that whip and swivel as the huge tires bounce over potholes in the road. They dress in spotted uniforms covered with outer layers of thick material which makes them move stiffly, robotically. They don full-cover helmets and goggles which hide their faces. Their weapons are lightweight and fire multiple rounds at incredible speed and velocity. They fly through the air in helicopters with guns and cannons which protruding from various parts of their black metal skins as they spit death and destruction at any moving thing they do not like.

And the people are terrified. They're not on the streets welcoming these creatures from another dimension. They hide in their homes, cringing in the corners or they flee to the mosque where they kneel and bow in prayer awaiting the apocalypse.

But the apocalypse never comes. Within hours, the foreigners are gone just as quickly as they arrived, like a hoard of locusts laving only dusts clouds and devastation behind them as they move north following the river toward the capital. Except for the funeral processions of the victims, by the next day, life has returned to normal.

But there has been a change in Fatimah. She no longer cleans. Now she sits, sometimes indoors, sometimes in the entrance way, sometimes on her haunches next to the road, waiting for…she is not sure what she is waiting for. She believes she will know the sign when it comes.

On the second day after the locusts have advanced through the town, the weather shifts, the winds blow from the north funneling down through the mountains picking up speed across the plains, gathering up sand from the desert, darkening the horizon, blocking out the rising sun.

Throughout the day, the storm blows. People shutter their homes and businesses. The market closes. If they must go out, people wrap themselves from head to toe in order to protect themselves from the stinging sand. There is no escape. The sand is everywhere.

Fatimah grows restless. She sits clawing at her clothes, her hair, her skin like a cat in heat. There is madness in her eyes which Muhammad cannot see because he cannot bear to look at her. And the winds continue to blow. All night. Into the next day.

"I do not remember a storm like this," says Muhammad.

Fatimah is ready to crawl out of her skin.

She feels like she's dying. She cannot understand why this man is talking to her. What is he saying? What does he mean?

"If the winds continue like this, it will take days to recover. I must go to the mosque and call people to prayer."

Fatimah only hears the man say he must go, and all she can think is yes, please go, go away, go away and leave me alone. Please go. And then she knows that she is alone. But calm does not return. She is still wild. She is being called. This is the sign. She will go with the wind.

Fatimah removes all of her clothes and stands naked in the middle of the room. Then she takes, in one hand, the sharp knife she uses to cut chickens and with the other hand she grasps her beautiful thick black hair. Then she slowly hacks away. The curls fall down, sliding across her body onto the floor. Then Fatimah takes a cloth, dips it in water and ritually cleanses her body, washing away all traces of hair, of him, of this house, of her current life. Her hands tremble as she rubs her neck, her breasts, her belly, between her legs, her thighs, her knees, her calves. She lifts each foot and wipes her ankles, her soles, between her toes. When she is finished, she breaths deeply three times.

She covers her nakedness with her thickest black abaya. She walks over to their bed. She spits on the bed. She walks to the entrance way. She spits on the jam. She opens the door and goes out into the winds. She turns and, as she closes the door behind her, spits on the door.

Then she leans forward *into* the face of the fierce storm and begins walking. She does not know where she is going.

She only knows she needs to go, forward *into* the wind. She knows she will never let herself be blown backward *by* the wind ever again.

When Muhammad comes back from the mosque, he knows she is gone. He searches for her, but he knows he will not find her. The winds die down. People return to the streets. The town comes back to life. But a part of Muhammad is dead.

Fatimah is gone.

The Sixth Day
Swept Away...

Muhammad awakens, still naked but not bound in any way. He sees that his head is not covered. Schatzi is gone, but in her place he finds orange coveralls, a bar of soap, a bucket of clean water and a broom.

Muhammad performs his ritual ablutions, then cleans his wounds as best he can. The soap burns his face even where his beard has grown back. He examines his right foot which remains tender and misshapen, but not unbearably painful to his touch. He tries on the coveralls, They fit reasonably well. He splashes the remaining water on the floor and, by limping about and leaning on the broom handle like a poor beggar in the marketplace, he sweeps his cell with the broom.

Just as he completes his tasks, he hears the call to prayer. He kneels and faces the direction pointed out to him by The Interrogator, but by the second bow, his routine is interrupted by the two guards entering his cell.

The guards drag Muhammad to the game room which has been temporarily transformed into a semblance of a military courtroom. Three officers, one of them being The Captain, sit behind a table at the front of the room. They are all very calm, even formal. The Captain's scar looks more dashing than menacing.

Muhammad is thrown down onto a chair to the left, facing the officers. To the right sits The Interrogator. Behind them sit other prisoners encircled by their guards.

The captain speaks: "This is not a trial. This is not a hearing. This is a voluntary gathering which will not determine the guilt or innocence of the accused. It is, if you will, a gathering to accuse the accused to determine if said accused is rightly accused and therefore properly held in detention. Furthermore, this gathering is not actually taking place as an actual gathering, it is more correctly described as a voluntary coming together of interested parties and neither the accused nor any other accused may claim precedent or rights based on this coming together. Order will be maintained at all times. Disorder will be punished severely. Begin!"

The Interrogator stands, and the three officers insert earphones for translation.

"On an unspecified date, some bad guys did a very bad thing at an unspecified checkpoint in the desert regions of an unspecified country. One unnamed man, perhaps a soldier, was killed. Another government employee who may, or who may not have been a soldier, was seriously wounded.

"Two days later, the accused, one Muhammad Shakir, was found wandering in the desert. He had no explanation for being there. His clothes were in tatters. His body exhibited the sorts of wounds consistent with proximate exposure to a very bad thing.

"Under intense questioning, the accused has denied any knowledge of the alleged very bad thing. On the other hand, the accused has indicated he is willing to be assigned guilt for the alleged very bad thing. Either way, the accused has been unwilling

to provide any information concerning the alleged very bad thing or his alleged whereabouts at the time the alleged very bad thing took place. We will, today, establish, for off-the-record documentation, in front of unnamed but actual witnesses, whether Muhammad Shakir should remain in custody for further questioning concerning the alleged very bad thing.

"Will Muhammad Shakir stand and identify himself before this voluntary gathering.

Muhammad stands, leaning against his chair.

"You are Muhammad Shakir?"

"I am who you say I am."

"That being Muhammad Shakir?"

"You have said it."

"Mr. Shakir, or should I address you as Imam Shakir?

"You may address me as you address me."

"Yes, well, uh…Muhammad, you heard my opening statement?"

"Yes."

"Is it accurate insofar as you have knowledge of the events described?"

"I have no knowledge of the events described."

"So…since you assert you have no knowledge of the alleged very bad thing and its aftermath of other bad things, then, as I asked, 'insofar as you have knowledge' my opening statement is correct?"

"I have no way of knowing if it is correct or incorrect."

"Have you or have you not, on various occasions, expressed to me your guilt about doing very bad things?"

"I have expressed guilt many times for many bad things, and, God willing, I hope my sins will be forgiven."

"Would it not also be a sin, a lie, to express guilt for doing a

very bad thing which you, in fact, did not do?"

"If I did not do the very bad thing it would be a lie. But if I did do the very bad thing, then it would not be a lie."

"Exactly! So let me ask you directly, are you one of the bad guys who did a very bad thing?"

"By what judgement would one decide who is a bad guy and who is a good guy?"

A number of the prisoners chuckle over Muhammad's verbal gymnastics. The Interrogator is clearly annoyed.

"Muhammad Shakir, I do not wish to persecute an innocent man. If you are innocent, help me set you free."

"I am already, absolutely free. It is you who are in prison."

Upon hearing these words, many of the prisoners clap and cheer, but when the guards train their weapons on the prisoners, the uproar quickly subsides.

"You make a mockery of this gathering."

"I mock no one."

"Do you want to undergo further interrogation?"

"Am I not now being interrogated?"

"Voluntarily. This is a voluntary gathering, Mr. Shakir."

The Interrogator has a thin, tight smile.

"Do you want to undergo further involuntary interrogation?"

"No,"

"Then tell us what we need to know."

"It appears you need to know many, things..."

"Mr. Shakir!"

"...and there are many, many more things you do not even know you do not know."

The prisoners clap and cheer and whistle before the guards wade in with their clubs. A mini-riot ensues. The officers use their chairs as shields and back out of the room facing unruly prisoners the way an animal trainer backs out of the tiger cage. Meanwhile the guards are cracking heads, punching stomachs and breaking bones. Crack! Smack! Thwak!

Amidst all this action, left alone and untouched, The Interrogator and Muhammad Shakir face each other. Neither flinches. Neither turns away.

Hours later, alone after being returned to his cell, Muhammad seeks guidance in prayer. Kneeling, his forehead pressed against the concrete, he petitions His God:

"Oh Merciful and Compassionate God, please let them end my life or set me free. I am not certain can stand more pain and abuse. In truth, Oh God, I am afraid. I cannot let them see my fear, but I am afraid. I do not want anymore of this…"

So engrossed was he in his prayers, that Muhammad did not hear The Interrogator enter his cell and he was unprepared for the kick which slammed into his left hip and sent him spinning up against the wall.

"You publicly humiliate me before the entire prison?"

Muhammad cowers against the wall rubbing his hip.

The Interrogator paces back and forth, his hands behind his back.

"I have tried to be your friend. I have tried to help you…"

His pace quickens.

"Take off the coveralls."

Muhammad slips out of his orange jumpsuit.

"Put this back on!"

Muhammad looks at his hood.

"Put it on!"

Muhammad places the hood over his head.

"Get down on the floor."

Muhammad returns to his knees, his head against the

floor, his arms folded against the back of his neck.

"Trust me Muhammad, you need me!"

Muhammad's muted voice escapes from beneath his chest.

"I place my trust in God, the Almighty and the Munificent."

This answer only further infuriates The Interrogator. He grabs the broom resting against the wall in Muhammad's cell raises it into the air and brings it down full force against Muhammad's back breaking the handle into two pieces. He then picks up one of the pieces and studies it. Then he moves over and kneels next to Muhammad.

"Talk to me…"

Muhammad is silent. The Interrogator is urgent.

"Please talk to me…"

Muhammad remains silent.

"Well, then, maybe this will loosen you up…"

The Interrogator presses the broom handle against Muhammad's rectum.

"…you tight-assed hadji."

The Interrogator shoves the wooden shaft up inside Muhammad.

"Aaaargh!"

"Try to fuck me over…"

The Interrogator moves the handle in and out of Muhammad simulating sexual penetration.

"…we'll see who gets fucked."

He makes a particularly violent thrust.

"Aaaargh!"

Muhammad's lips move silently.

I have asked You to let me be free, instead You bring me more pain. I seek peace; You bring me violence. I am honored that You have chosen me…

The Interrogator continues to violate Muhammad with even greater intensity. Sweat beads form on his face and arms. His eyes are closed. The veins in his neck bulge.

...but if I am the chosen sacrifice, then give me strength to endure... Uh!

The Interrogator pushes deep.

...the strength to give all that I am in service to You, my God, in service to You, the Source of all hope, in service to You so that the world can be a better place...and...and in sacrifice...

"Aaaargh! Aaaargh!"

The Interrogator twists and shakes, then slumps onto his knees.

There is blood on the broom handle. Blood seeping from Muhammad, but Muhammad is silent. There are no tears in his eyes.

The only tears being shed are those in the eyes of The Interrogator as he drops the wooden shaft and stares at his trembling hands.

The Sixth Memory
The Fire Fight...

Fatimah walks for three days and four nights without stopping to eat or even to rest. Finally, at dawn on the morning of the fourth day, she drops to the ground, exhausted, and falls asleep under the roof of an abandoned warehouse in a complex of abandoned ware- houses not five kilometers from the outskirts of the very town she has fled. In her desperation and confusion, she has all along been wandering in circles.

Fatimah's abandonment of her life with Muhammad causes subtle but noticeable changes in Muhammad. Not so much aggressive, as less gentle. Not so much bitter, as less happy. His long, lanky body grows stiff and slightly bent. His smooth skin develops rashes and blemishes. His bright eyes are of- ten vacant, cloudy, distant.

And his sermons are punctuated with barbed attacks on the foreign invaders even while his overall message remains conciliatory. After one such sermon, he receives a visit from Sheik Majih who nervously warns Muhammad that he and the other elders do not approve of the path certain words of Muhammad's appear to have taken.

"And of what path do you speak, Sheik Majih?"

"The path of anger and resentment."

"And we should not feel anger and resentment over what has happened?"

The sheik takes a string of beads from his pocket and maneuvers the beads back and forth with his gnarled bony fingers while he considers his next question. Finally he asks, "Anger and resentment over what the foreigners are doing or over what someone else has done to you?"

Muhammad is stunned. "You mean?

"Fatimah is gone."

"Yes."

"A man needs a wife."

"Yes."

"Without her, he can become…"

"I see the direction of your thoughts, Sheik Majih, but I do not want to speak of Fatimah, nor do I believe my remarks concerning the foreigners are affected by the fact that my wife has left for the capital to visit with her ailing aunt."

"Her aunt."

"Her ailing aunt."

"Who will survive her illness, God willing."

"Yes…God willing."

The sheik continues to play with his beads while he judges the most effective approach to convince Muhammad he should tone down his sermons. Finally he decides to speak directly.

"You serve at our discretion, Imam Muhammad,"

"And at your pleasure, Sheik Majih."

"The invaders will soon be our rulers…at least for the foreseeable future. It is not in our interests, certainly not in your interests, to antagonize them."

"Are we such jackals?"

Now the sheik is angry. "Our time will come, Muhammad Shakir, but in the meantime, we do not want trouble. Do as I say, or you will find yourself without a position here. Is that understood?"

"Yes, I understand."

And so Muhammad complies with the directives of the elders, not by speaking kindly about the foreigners, but by not speaking about them at all.

Meanwhile, Fatimah awakens to find herself surrounded by men in black. Someone is pushing forward from the back of the group. As he makes his way past the others into the inner circle, Fatimah sees that someone is Hakim. As he bends down and lifts her off the ground, she wraps her arms around his neck.

When she looks into Hakim's eyes, she knows she has found her way to a new life. All of the tension and stress and guilt she has been hoarding in her lost soul comes pouring out of her. Not in tears. But in smiles and short outbursts of genuine laughter. And then she discovers her newly acquired freedom allows her to speak again. "How did you find me?" she asks Hakim.

"It is you who found us," he says smiling at her, "and I will not let you go back…ever."

He carries Fatimah deeper into the complex, then down a flight of stairs through a long tunnel. They emerge into a cavernous chamber carved out of the bedrock. The room is filled with cardboard boxes and wooden crates and steel shipping containers. Along the far side of the cave are a series of rooms where the rebels have established living quarters. Hakim carries Fatimah into his room and gently lays her down on his cot.

"Why didn't you tell me?"

"Tell you?"

"About our baby?"

"So you know…how…of course, when you talked with Muhammad." She is thoughtful. "I cannot explain why I didn't tell you. I could not. I could not talk to anyone. I thought I was dead too."

"And the foreigners' bomb ended it's life?"

"Yes."

"One more thing to remember…" He looks away. His jaw twitches, but he maintains control.

"Yes," says Fatimah. She grabs his arm and squeezes it in her grasp. "That is why I want to join you," says Fatimah. "I want to fight them. I want to kill them."

"It is not an easy way to live, Fatimah. And most of us will die."

Fatimah turns away. "I have already died once and been reborn. It cannot be so hard the second time."

Hakim laughs. "Well, I will do my best to make sure you do not find out a second time." He kisses her on the forehead. "Now you must rest," he whispers, "and grow strong." He kisses her again, but she is already drifting off into a deep sleep.

While Fatimah sleeps, Muhammad lies awake. He cannot sleep for any length of time. Occasionally, he grows so drowsy he nods off only to have his head jerk forward, his eyes flicker open and his consciousness slowly reemerge with the drool which has gathered on his chin.

As he wanders through his mosque's courtyard preparing for his Friday sermon, Muhammad asks God to show him the way.

"All praise be to You, My God, Who is My Light in the Darkness, now give me the strength to understand. You have taken so much from me—my father, my child, my wife, and yet I still honor You, praise You, obey You. Am I crazy? Am I a fool?"

He sits for a moment on the stone bench near the lemon tree. He sees a column of ants marching from their nest, and another column returning. He remembers when he was a child listening to the old women at the well talking about him. He had squashed hundreds if not thousands of ants that day for no reason any ant would understand.

He asks God: "Am I an ant? Am I being squashed for Your amusement? Or are You angry with me? Am I being punished?"

In his frustration, Muhammad kicks at the outgoing ant column which scatters in random disarray. He shakes his fist in the air. "My God, My God…why? I have always been faithful to You! I have been Your faithful ant!" He returns his gaze to the ground. The ants have already reestablished their relentless journey along their chosen path. Muhammad shakes his head, resigned. He will follow the path laid out for him.

On his walk home, a convoy of foreign soldiers in their monster vehicles passes him by on the main road. Just as the last vehicle, a supply truck, roars past, there's a tremendous Boom! A personnel carrier flies into the air riding atop an orange and red ball of fire. Then the vehicle, spouting smoke and flames, slams back to the ground scattering soldiers and their supplies across the highway.

As Muhammad watches the spectacle, shots are fired from

a low wall behind him and to his right. Other soldiers in the convoy return fire toward the wall, and Muhammad finds himself in the middle of a fire fight as he throws himself on the ground while bullets whistle overhead.

Muhammad is sweating . His hands are shaking, his ears are ringing, he looks for an escape. He sees a depression, a drainage ditch ten meters ahead and so he forces himself to slowly crawl forward toward the ditch. Although bullets strike the ground very near him, and he winces each time, he eventually manages to reach the ditch without being shot. He rolls down the embankment and breaths a huge sigh.

But Muhammad's relief is short lived. Not three meters away from him lies someone dressed in black, pressed to the ground, with a cell phone in the person's right hand.

Then Muhammad sees one of the foreign soldiers running toward the ditch, his weapon raised in firing position. When the soldier also throws himself into the trench, Muhammad decides to scurry back out preferring to take his chances on the open ground, but when he realizes the soldier is going to shoot the figure in black. He yells: "Watch out! Behind you, my brother."

The soldier's attention shifts to Muhammad who immediately raises his arms in the air when he sees the soldier's weapon pointed at him. The figure in black quickly rolls over, produces a handgun and fires. Muhammad sees the soldier's face shatter into broken bone, blood and bits of flesh as the rest of his body crumples to the ground.

Muhammad turns toward the figure in black who's wearing a ski mask. Suddenly his already precarious psyche receives another jolt—he knows those eyes! He blurts out: "Fatimah?"

She can only stare back at him. "Fatimah…what…?"

Fatimah shakes her head, and signals for Muhammad to get down lower just as another hail of bullets flies over them,

Muhammad ignores her warning and crawls over to her.

"Fatimah…"

The figure in black turns away from Muhammad. "I am not Fatimah. My name is Ishtar, warrior goddess, wife of Ashur."

"You are fighting for the resistance?"

"I am the avenging angel of death."

She reaches for her cell phone and dials a number. Suddenly the ground rumbles and there's another enormous explosion even greater than the first one which sent the personnel carrier flying through the air. Secondary explosions! Thumps and crashes! Muhammad hears the screams of the wounded and the dying. A massive cloud of thick, black smoke fills the air.

Fatimah rises to her knees. "Come…now. We have to get out of here…now!"

Fatimah pulls on Muhammad's arm as they scurry up the side of the ditch and run across the open ground toward the wall. A few shots ring out from the convoy. They are answered by a volley from behind the wall just as Muhammad and Fatimah leap over the top and land in a heap on the other side.

Muhammad takes a moment to catch his breath. Then he rolls over to try and talk to Fatimah, but she is already running toward the other black-clad figures who are retreating into the town.

Muhammad calls out: "Fatimah!" but by then, she has turned a corner and disappeared.

Suddenly there is renewed firing from the direction of the bombed-out convoy. Muhammad peeks over he wall.

The soldiers are gathering their dead and wounded, and then scrambling into their undamaged vehicles which roar off leaving the burning carcasses of the damaged trucks behind.

As soon as they're gone, a steady stream of young men and boys come running from the town toward the highway. They dance around the wrecks, raising their scavenged pieces of twisted metal toward the sky and chanting, "Death to the foreigners! Death to the infidels!" while the plume of greasy black smoke provides a beacon for the helicopter gunship swooping down upon the scene.

When the gunship fires its cannons and machine guns, dozens of the revelers are hit and go down. But, instead of intimidating the others, the firing from the gunship only increases their furry and their frenzy. And even more young men join the mob. One of the young men has a rocket launcher. After numerous attempts to properly rest the weapon on his shoulder, he launches a grenade toward one of the gunships and scores an unlikely hit.

More flames! More explosions! Another huge crash! The crowd surges forward and pulls the wounded from the downed helicopter. Then Muhammad watches in horror as the bodies of the survivors are hacked and torn apart. Then he sees young boys, children really, set the body pieces on fire and then carry the charred remains about on poles like trophies.

Muhammad sees war at its most basic and primitive. And it sickens him. He returns to his mosque and prepares his sermon.

The Seventh Day
Taking a Beating...

The fat rat gets fatter during the night, feasting on the fresh blood seeping from the rectum of the naked man collapsed on the floor. At first, the rat moves cautiously. The scent of the dog is still in the air, and the scents of an anger and fear, but after his various probes encounter no activity other than moans and groans from the unconscious body offering up such delicacies, the rat is free to eat his fill.

Then the screams begin. Deep, wounded, piercing screams from the heart and soul of the abused prisoner. The rat scampers away, back inside the walls, safe from the ear splitting wails.

I hear the screaming again. I cannot sleep. I cannot rest until this screaming stops.

It seems so close. At most, the screaming prisoner is in a cell near mine. More likely, right next to mine. Yes, the screaming must be coming from the cell right next to me.

The noise is terrible! Terrible! If I did not know better, I would say the noise is coming from my own cell. From…

Ah . Yes. So now I know the truth…the screaming is coming from my own cell, from my own body…from me!

And with that admission, the longest, loneliest, most painful wail of all goes forth from the cell of Muhammad Shakir and echoes through the hallways of the prison causing all who hear it to shudder and shake with dread and despair.

It is The Corporal who draws the assignment to come and check on Muhammad who remains on the floor. Naked. Bleeding. With- out his hood. He awakens and sees her standing, leaning against the wall, looking down at him. He makes no attempt to cover himself, to cover his cock or his balls. He is content to watch her watching him. Content to study her eyes as her eyes study the various wounds, scabs and scars on his body.

The corporal speaks to Muhammad.

"Look what you've made them do to you. Oh…my… God…

"I've heard the stories about you. They say you can overcome the dogs, outsmart The Interrogator, withstand ungodly amounts torture and abuse. You're a big deal around here, ya' know that?"

Muhammad cannot understand a word, but he senses her tone is not hostile.

"And even I dream about you. You are always in my dreams. Your ugly awful face next to mine…your ugly lips on mine…and your beautiful, sorrowful dark eyes with long lashes searching mine…I hate you're fucking guts…and I love you…I hate you're fucking guts…and I love you"

The Corporal is crying.

Muhammad pulls himself up and slowly limps over toward her. As he looks into her eyes and tries to express his portion of the pain they share, he lets the tips of his fingers softly slide down her cheek to her chin.

"May the peace of God be with you."

But his haunting voice and his tender gesture break The Corporal's last connection to her sanity. She slaps Muhammad, becomes hysterical and runs from his cell holding her hands over her ears; and swaying from side to side, she stumbles down the corridor.

Within minutes other guards arrive lead by The Captain and the acne-pocked Muscleman who swore vengeance against Muhammad,

The Captain's scar shines red, the rest of his pale face flushed pink. The private is ready to throw his weight around as he strokes his right bicep and clenches, unclenches, clenches again his fist.

"I've had enough of The Interrogator's methods," says The Captain, "Now we use mine."

The short Muscleman steps forward, draws back and smashes his fist full force into Muhammad's face, breaking Muhammad's nose and sending him sprawling back onto the floor.

Aaaagh, ah, that really hurt! I wonder how much of this I can take. I will have to give them something or they will surely beat me to death. What should I say when The Interrogator arrives?

But The Interrogator does not arrive, and the contingent in Muhammad's cell has no intention of questioning him at all. The Muscleman lifts Muhammad up, draws back again and this time slams his fist into Muhammad's jaw. The crunch of bones breaking cuts through the air. Then the thump! thump! thump! as The Muscleman kicks Muhammad in the head and stomach.

Fatimah! Mother Marium! God of Heaven and Earth they no longer want me alive. I am meant for death, I know this now.

There is nothing I can say. Nothing I can do to make this bitter tea pass from lips and be consumed by another...

The Captain becomes, if anything, even more enraged by blood lust and power. He pulls The Muscleman back and takes a few good kicks himself. Then he grabs Muhammad's left wrist, forces Muhammad's left hand flat on the floor and stomps on it with his heel, Muhammad's fingers crack.

...but there is no other to drink from this cup. You have chosen me...You have...chosen... Aaaagh...But if You are all merciful and compassionate, why do I have to suffer such pain? Can I not just let my world go dark and join You in Heaven? What is gained by...Aaaagh!

The Captain breaks the fingers in Muhammad's other hand. "Oooohal!" A vicious kick to the ribs brings other broken bones.

The Muscleman has produced a whip which he uses to scourge Muhammad's back and shoulders. Angry red welts become bloody wounds. Bits of torn flesh are ripped away.

Muhammad collapses on the floor, his breathing is heavy, labored, his skin turning pale from loss of blood. The Captain stands over him. His breathing is equally heavy, but his trauma comes from the exaltation of dominance and the extinction of another human life.

The Muscleman continues to flail away on Muhammad's body even though Muhammad has nothing left to give. The expanding bulge in the crotch of The Muscleman's pants leaves little doubt as to the sorts of pleasure he is experiencing. His moans and grunts each time the whip descends again confirm his mounting orgasm.

"Ooooha!"

"Ride 'em, cowboy!"

Just as the frenzy nears its peak, The Interrogator does appear. He surveys all that is going on. "Stop!"

The Muscleman holds the whip over his head. The Captain whirls around, curious to see who has issued the command. When he sees The Interrogator, he is furious.

"You can't issue a contradictory order. I outrank you!"

"With all do respect, not in this part of the prison, sir. You are aware of the chain of command in the hadji wing."

"Yes."

"Then leave me alone with the prisoner…and take your freak with you," he says pointing to The Muscleman, "You've done enough damage for one day."

"Damage? Damage! Someone has to reassert control."

"He was ready to talk, you fool. He was totally humiliated and shamed. Now…now it's only physical pain. He can deal with that."

"They must all be destroyed. Obliterated from the face of the earth. Our civilization depends on it."

"If your civilization is dependant on the eradication of those who oppose you, then your civilization cannot survive. Your civilization will only survive if enough of those who oppose you end up wanting to be you."

"Blabber on…blabber, blabber, blabber…"

"You walk close to the line, sir."

The Captain takes The Interrogator's warning seriously. He signals for The Muscleman to follow him as he heads for the door. "He's a dead man either way."

"Dead men can't tell their secrets, Captain." The interrogator turns his attention to Muhammad.

"So…let's see if you're still alive."

Muhammad opens his eyes.

"Good, Good. There is still time."

The interrogator sits down next to Muhammad and places Muhammad's bloody head on his lap. He places his finger on Muhammad's neck to check for a pulse. He smiles. Stronger than he would have assumed. He shakes his head, marvelling at how Muhammad seems to be able to withstand anything.

Muhammad drifts off under The Interrogator's protection.

The end draws near. I know no fear because You are with me, My Lord, My God, Creator of all that is good in this world. My Hope, the Hope of Nations. The Hope of the World! All praise be to You, Oh God, for there is no God but God…

The interrogator watches Muhammad's face, the eyes darting back and forth beneath their lids, the twitches, the trembling lips forming the silent words of a comforting prayer…

…I await with joy my passage into Your Kingdom where I can see in the light of Your Light, bask in the warmth in the heat of Your Sun, bath in the sweet cool waters of Your Fountain. And I shall hear the angels singing, their voices raised in praise to Thee, and I shall hear one million million prayers chanted in praise of Thee, and I shall hear Your Voice reach out to all and bring comfort and joy and peace, yes, Dear God, please, peace…

The Interrogator brushes back a strand of hair which has fallen across Muhammad's forehead. Again he whispers:

"There is still time."

The Seventh Memory
A Warrior Princess...

Muhammad looks out at the men gathered before him, and begins to speak:

"God is great. He is compassionate and merciful. He is the Protector of our land, the Hope of our future. We praise our Lord God and beseech Him to hear our voices raised in prayer during these terrible times.

"I cannot condemn the horror I myself saw on the road to Najaf. Have the foreign devils not brought this upon themselves? Have they not broken into our homes? Violated our women? Killed our children? Destroyed our businesses? Even defiled our holy places? Do they not deserve to die?"

There are murmurs from those gathered.

"And is the manner of their dying of any importance? Is the desecration of their bodies a sin? These are difficult questions for we do have cause…We have cause."

The young men nod in agreement. Others lower their heads in contemplation. Many elders shake their heads in opposition to Muhammad's words.

"We have cause, my brothers, because the foreigners have gorged themselves on our treasure, on our bounty, on our blood. They have filled themselves without fear of reprisal. They are the fattened hogs ready to be butchered. And our butchering knives are ready, sharp as razors, strong as tempered steel. And we will use them. We have cause." The young men leap to their feet. They are cheering and clapping, urging Imam Muhammad Shakir forward.

"We have cause to take life because so many lives have been taken from us. How many foreign lives equal the life of one of our precious, innocent babies? How many foreigners should die to make up for the poor grandfather shot as he rested on the steps of his very own house where he had lived for seventy-three years? How many foreign bodies should be burned to balance the raging fire storms which consume whole families, entire neighborhoods? I have no pity for the infidels. We have cause."

This time some of the fence sitter and even a few of the elders are on their feet praising Muhammad and chanting, "Death to the foreigners! Death to the infidels!" The walls of the mosque echo with angry voices declaring opposition toward the invaders and support for Muhammad.

"So what if our cause haunts our every sleeping moment? So what if our cause brutalizes us so that we abuse each other? So what if our cause turns us all into hyenas, jackals feasting on the rotting carcass of our despair? We have cause!"

As these words sink in, the celebrator y mood diminishes.

"Yesterday I saw the beast. He does not travel in monster truck convoys. He does not march in camouflage uniforms and bulletproof vests. He does not fly in gunships spewing fire from the sky. I saw the beast…and he is us."

Shouts of "No! No!" from some. Others have grown quite somber. Some who were only seconds earlier nodding their heads in agreement, now look puzzled, their eyes filled with doubt.

"Must we become the beast in order to kill the beast? We have cause. We do have cause. I cannot judge. But God also offers us another path, another way. For it is written: '...if you pardon and forbear and forgive, then surely God is Forgiving, Merciful...'."

More agreement from those gathered around Muhammad. A few remaining shouts of dissent.

"We have released the beast within us. We are prowling the same killing ground in the same manner as the foreign invaders. Is this how we serve a merciful and compassionate God?"

The gathered faithful have now united behind their imam.

"Let us bring our beast back inside its cage. Let it be said we walk above, not beside or below these running dogs for in the end, once this war has ended, we will be masters of our domain and the foreign devils, a distant memory.

"There is no God but God, Praise God!"

After the applause has diminished and Muhammad has moved off to the side while the men break into smaller groups to debate and discuss the merits of his sermon, Sheik Majih approaches Muhammad and kisses him on both cheeks.

"You spoke well, Imam Muhammad Shakir."

"Thank you, Sheik Majih."

"We are pleased and hope your wise words will calm the younger men."

"And I hope my words please God."

"I am sure they do, but the events of yesterday will bring the wrath of the occupation upon us if we do not appear calm and repentant."

"I would wish to avoid that."

Sheik Majih hesitates for some time before he looks Muhammad straight in the eye. "It is said that your wife, Fatimah, is with them. That she lives with their leader in a compound outside the city."

"I have heard this."

"She calls herself Ishtar, after the warrior goddess, sworn to vengeance."

"So it is said."

"And you allow this?"

"She is not under my command."

"She is your wife."

"In name only."

"These insurgents must be stopped."

"Why tell me this?"

"She is your wife. We need an emissary to speak with them. You will be our emissary."

Three days later Muhammad finds himself trudging under the blazing noonday sun toward the abandoned warehouses where he had been told he will be met by a guide from the insurgents, but as he enters the grounds the only living things he sees are lizards and flies. The only sounds he hears are the winds whistling through the skeletons of the broken and abandoned structures.

He stands, waiting. Still, no one appears. He moves to a shack which has no walls, but it's corrugated metal roof provides some shade. He sits. He waits. There is no one. Nothing.

Muhammad decides to leave. Just as he passes the last building, a figure in black appears and signals Muhammad should follow him. Soon, they are joined by others. Then they stop and Muhammad is blindfolded. Then he finds himself descending stairs. The air grows cooler. More stairs. Then a long walk. They stop. A door opens. They walk forward. The door shuts behind them. The blindfold is removed.

Muhammad finds himself standing before Hakim who is seated behind a table in small room where there are three or four other chairs. Hakim indicates Muhammad should sit down. Then Hakim speaks: "Imam Muhammad, you bring messages from the elders of the town."

"Yes."

"Well, what do the rabbits want to say to us?"

"They want you to stop fighting. They want you to turn in your weapons."

"Seriously?"

"That is what they want. In return…"

"Yes. What do they offer in return?"

"They will give you amnesty. They will protect you from the foreign devils."

Hakim slaps the pistol on his waist. "We can protect ourselves."

"For now, until they descend on you like well-armed locusts."

"Then we shall die a martyr's death, no? You can make us heroes in your sermons."

Muhammad looks around at the others in the room. They are all wearing masks. He turns back to Hakim. "Where is Fatimah?"

"There is no one here called Fatimah."

"I saved her life in the trench. I would like to speak to her."

One of the black-clad figures steps forward. Muhammad studies the eyes. It is Fatimah.

"Go home, Muhammad. We are no longer man and wife. I want to be here. Divorce me. It is over."

"You will die here."

"I was dying with you."

Hakim interrupts. "We are not here to settle your domestic disputes, Muhammad."

"I agree."

There's a long silence. Hakim's eyes bore into Fatimah. Fatimah steps back.

Hakim shrugs. "Then, to the issue at hand. Tell the elders…tell them if they want their dignity, their self-respect, they should send all their young men to fight with us. Then, when victory is won, we will grant them amnesty."

"There is nothing else?"

"No."

"Then I will go and tell them you are prepared to fight to the end?"

"To the end…our victory will be victory for all the people."

As Muhammad trudges back toward town, he is overtaken by a lone figure in black. He stops. It is Fatimah. She removes her mask.

"I am sorry I spoke those words, Muhammad. It is not your fault."

"You are with Hakim, sorry Ashur?"

"It is not about Hakim,"

"He once raped you."

"Yes."

"Yes? That's all you have to say?"

"It is complicated."

"Do you now love him?"

"I am finished with love. I only seek revenge."

"That is a bitter pill."

"I am a bitter woman."

"Peace be with you, Fatimah." He kisses her on both cheeks.

"And with you, Muhammad." She turns and heads back toward the compound.

When Muhammad reports back to the elders, they are very disappointed. And, they are caught in a bind. If they appear to side with the foreigners, they will lose their children for the young do not want their country ruled by the invaders. If they stand up to the invaders, they will lose their town to death and destruction.

Sheik Wahad Majih asks Imam Muhammad Shakir to accompany him when he goes to speak with the local commander of the occupying forces at the invaders' dusty, desert base 15 kilometers south of their town.

They travel in the Sheik's car, an ancient Mercedes diesel belching black smoke as they rumble toward Camp Liberty Rising, a modest collection of tents, tanks and other vehicles surrounded by a massive earthen berm the foreigners have bulldozed into place in order to protect them from attack, Even before the Mercedes can approach the camp's gate, Muhammad and Sheik Majih are stopped by various other barriers and checkpoints. Then, at the gate, they are told to leave the car outside and approach on foot.

While the base is not large, both Muhammad and the sheik are impressed by the stockpiles of arms and machinery inside. As the two, in their turbans and flowing robes, are escorted to the office of Colonel A. Douglas Winthrob by their Arabic-speaking interpreter, dozens and dozens of soldiers in desert camouflage scurry about. One tall, raw-boned fellow approaches and asks, If he “can have the interpreter take his picture with two honest-to-God real natives.” Muhammad and the sheik have no objection, so the soldier gets his souvenir—a photo of himself standing between, and towering over, two men in tribal dress. Only a close inspection of the picture draws one's attention to the soldier's hands where each displays an extended index finger

Colonel Winthrob turns out to be a cordial man with an austere office consisting of a desk, a computer, wall maps of the area, a few bookshelves and a motley collection of metal chairs. He is medium in all things, height, weight, fitness, accomplishments. His only distinguishing characteristic is a large, drooping mustache that occasionally, from a distance, makes people think he's a local policeman.

“Drink? No, of course not, what am I thinking, heh, heh…well, sit, sit, please.” After Muhammad and the sheik have been seated, the colonel then sits behind his desk. “So, sheik Mahji, what is on our agenda for today?”

Although Sheik Mahji speaks the foreign tongue, he prefers to work though an interpreter, and is forced to do so with Muhammad in the room. When the interpreter is finished, the sheik responds: “Thank you, Colonel Winthrob for taking time from your busy schedule to meet with us. I would like to discuss the situation with the insurgents. I have brought with me the imam of our local mosque, Imam Muhammad Shakir, who has recently met with the rebels.”

The colonel turns his attention to Muhammad. “You met with this Ashur and his crew? What did you think of them?”

“They are very dedicated.”

“Dedicated…hummm, yes. So where did you meet them?”

"I was blindfolded during the last part of my journey."

"Where did you make contact with them?"

"I…would prefer not to say."

The Colonel turns to Sheik Mahji. "'He prefers not to say…' Why have you brought this man with you, sheikie, baby? He protects the enemy. Our common enemy."

"He has preached before the town in our favor, Colonel Winthrob. He has also lost an unborn child to one of your bombs…and, in a manner of speaking, a wife."

The Colonel returns to Muhammad. "I am sorry about that. I truly am. What do you figure they're worth? Couple thousand of our dollars? We could manage that…Now, where did they contact you."

Muhammad is speechless.

The Colonel is back on Sheik Mahji. "Sheikie, this is going nowhere. The insurgents must be eliminated. I could throw your imam here in prison, but I'm not going to do that right now. I want you both to think about…uhmmm, about consequences, yes, consequences. Do you understand?"

"Yes. Consequences."

"Anything else? How're the plans for the base versus town soccer match coming along? Getting nervous? We got some brown boys native to the game."

"Nothing new."

"Well then, "the Colonel stands abruptly, "until next time. I want peace for you…"

"And peace be to you also, Colonel"

As the old Mercedes pulls away from the base and heads back to town, Sheik Mahji turns to Muhammad. "You must make one last attempt to convince the insurgents to stop fighting."

"He mentioned 'consequences.' What did he mean?"

"We do not want to know, Muhammad Shakir. We do not want to know."

The Eighth Day
Breakthrough...

The prisoner Shakir sleeps fitfully on the floor in his empty cell. His body has been cleaned; his cell washed down. He is naked and his head is again covered by a hood.

It is a quiet morning. There is no screaming. Muhammad awakens with the morning call to prayer, but finds even the slightest movement virtually impossible, so he nods his head three times as he lies there and acknowledges his praise for his God.

Minutes later, his cell door opens and a short intense man wearing thick horn rimmed glasses and a thick white mustache barges in. There's a stethoscope hanging from around his neck and his white coat almost reaches the floor as he bows slightly and then brusquely greets Muhammad in his own language.

"Peace be with you."

Muhammad nods.

The examination proceeds very slowly once the doctor realizes the serious damage Muhammad has absorbed. He is especially concerned about internal injuries, and he asks numerous questions:

"Does it hurt here? Does it hurt there? Is this place tender? Do you feel pain when I touch you here? There? Can you swallow? Urinate? Do you see blood in your urine? Have you had a bowel movement? Is there blood in your feces?"

To all of these inquiries, Muhammad can only nod or shake his head. He tries to speak, but it is too painful. Meanwhile, from the doctor, there is a great deal of tisk-tisking, head shaking and even the occasional expletive. He is clearly not happy with what he discovers with each new probe of Muhammad. Finally, he sighs, and stands up, his chin resting on his right hand.

"You have suffered much, my friend. Why didn't you tell them what they want to know?"

Muhammad shakes his head.

"A true believer. What a shame. You won't last the week, I'm fairly certain. Are you prepared for what is coming?"

Muhammad nods.

"Well, okay then. I hope your paradise is real, and that you enter it soon, my brother."

Muhammad smiles.

The doctor reaches into his pocket and extracts a syringe.

"I can give you something for the pain. It might also allow you to speak. It will surely encourage you to return to sleep."

Muhammad shakes his head, refusing the injection, but the doctor administers the syringe anyway.

Muhammad sleeps. There are no dreams or visions.

When Muhammad awakens again, his hood had been removed. The Interrogator is in his cell, waiting patiently. When he sees Muhammad's eyes are open, he nods.

"Can you speak?"

Muhammad clears his throat, dribbles spittle, clears his

throat again. He tries to open his mouth, but he can't. He speaks with his mouth open only a crack, and produces a croaking sound. He clears his throat once more, and speaks without moving his jaw.

"I can. But…my jaw is broken."

"We do not have much time."

Muhammad smiles. *"I do not have much time."*

"As you wish."

The Interrogator shifts his weight. *"Can I get you anything?"*

"Water."

The Interrogator calls on his phone. Water arrives. And ice chips. The Interrogator moves and sits beside Muhammad. He cradles Muhammad's head in his lap and forces a few of the ice chips into Muhammad's mouth.

Ah. This is heavenly! Thank you, God, for showing some mercy in this moment. I never knew ice could…be so nice? Ah. Yes. An ice poem. Ice is nice. Better than rice. Can't eat lice. This will suffice. Ice is so nice. Now I have said it twice. Must be the drug that doctor gave me.

"Who are you protecting?"

Muhammad shakes his head.

"Another Imam?"

Muhammad shakes his head.

"A member of your tribe?"

Muhammad shakes his head.

"A local official?"

Muhammad shakes his head.

"Yourself, then. You're protecting yourself."

Muhammad nods his head.

"But…then you are guilty. You did do it."

Muhammad nods as vigorously as he is able.

"Why?"

Muhammad sighs.

The Interrogator presses a few more ice chips through Muhammad's lips.

"Have I not been good to you?"

Muhammad does not react.

"Trust me. It could have been much worse."

Muhammad shrugs.

"I believe you. I believe you did it. But I need to know why. Our files are correct. You really are an Imam. Why would you become a suicide bomber?"

Muhammad shrugs.

"You must tell me. It will make your end so much easier to bear."

Muhammad struggles to speak.

"I cannot."

"Why?"

"I do not know."

"You don't know why you can't tell me, or you don't know why you did it?"

"I don't know anything…when I dream…" Muhammad can barely get the words out. *"…I remember things. Maybe, before I die, I will know what happened.…Maybe not."*

"You remember nothing about that day?"

"That is true."

"Then you are of no more use to me."

"So be it,"

The Interrogator replaces Muhammad's hood.

"I am sorry."

He leaves Muhammad alone.

Muhammad is lost in his thoughts.

If they kill me now…when they kill me now…how will they kill me? That is the hardest part about dying. I do not want more pain. I am truly sick of the pain.

I know I go to a far, far better place than this, and I will not miss, much…most of what I leave behind. My homeland is worn and tired, exhausted from so many years of blood and oil and killing…always killing…more and more killing. They say even I have become one of the killers? Did I kill? Could I kill? Killing. The killing. So…how will I die?

Will they shoot me? What if they miss at first? Will they smother me? How can I force myself not to struggle? Will they gas me? That might not be so bad. Will I smell it? Electrocution? I do not like that idea at all.

And what will it be like to die? I mean, before I am with God? Will everything just go blank like when the TV goes off the air at night? Or when the power goes off? Will I still feel part of me? Will I feel myself leaving me? Will I know the way?

I must prepare myself. How long will they give me? Days? Hours? I am scared. I truly am scared. But I will not let them see my fear. I will not!

It is dark. Muhammad's cell door opens. The Muscleman and The Corporal enter and close the door behind them.

The corporal whispers: "Hey, Pssst…hey you! It's me."

Muhammad hears her and recognizes her voice if not the words.

"I brought a friend. Wanna' have a party?" She crawls over to him and grabs his cock.

She kisses it and is pleased to see it grow.

"You know me…you know me…" she purrs.

Muhammad is wary, He thinks this is the beginning of his death watch, but why would they be teasing him sexually?

Still, he is man, despite all that has happened, he is a man. And so he grows in spite of himself.

Suddenly The Corporal stops her purring. First, she rips off his hood. Then Muhammad finds himself turned over on his stomach, and rough calloused hands grasp his hips. He is in agony.

"Aaaagh!"

He hears The Corporal giggling, but she is not touching him.

The Muscleman spreads Muhammad's buttocks, then rams his stiff hard cock into Muhammad's anus.

"Ooooha!"

The corporal is giggling.

The Muscleman is sweating. "Ooooha! Ooooha!"

Muhammad screams.

"Aaaagh! Aaaagh!"

The corporal takes out a camera. Flash! The harsh strobe captures The Muscleman in mid-thrust. Flash! The Muscleman slaps Muhammad's hips. Flash! Flash! Flash!

The corporal's giggles turn to cackles of delight as she records the sordid scene. She bounds around the flailing bodies like a young baboon trying to get its share of the tribe's meal.

The Muscleman's rape grows even more aggressive and rapid. His breath comes in short bursts, his thrusts deeper, his grip tighter…

"OOOoooha!"

"AAAaaagh!"

And then it is over.

The corporal scitters around taking pictures of the walls and door and floor, anything to make the bright white light flash one more time.

Then The Interrogator enters. He shoos the others away. The Muscleman holds his hand out to The Corporal and they laugh as they head for the door.

The Interrogator and Muhammad are alone again.

"That's how bad it can get, Muhammad Shakir."

Muhammad is crying.

"The pictures will turn out great. You're the star."

Muhammad's sobs grow more intense.

"There is still time…there is still time…"

Muhammad breaks down completely.

"Talk to me."

"I did not kill anyone."

"We know this."

"I tried…I tried…"

Muhammad is crying again.

"You tried what?"

"I tried to stop her."

"Her?"

"Fatimah…my wife."

"Your wife carried the bomb?"

"Yes. I think so."

"Did she act alone?"

"Alone? No. She is the leader of her group."

"Hadji?"

"No. She does not believe…anymore."

"In God?"

"In God…or us. She believes in nothing."

"Who are the others?"

Muhammad sighs. He is loosing consciousness. His breathing is shallow.

"The young ones."

"Names."

"They are the nameless ones. The destroyed. The ruined. The abandoned."

"Why are they with her?"

"She has become their mother,"

"Their mother?"

"You took her natural child...our child."

Muhammad is crying again. Softly. Mournfully. Lonely.

"Where is she now?"

"I do not know."

"Finish your confession. It is good for you."

"I do not know."

"It is the last thing I need to know. You will be free."

"They live in the desert. Away from the city."

"Where."

"An oasis. South of Hallah."

"Thank you, Muhammad."

"Kill me now."

"Not now."

"Please."

"There is no need."

Muhammad's voice is barely audible. *"I have the need. Please...please..."*

The Interrogator places the hood back over Muhammad's head.

"Sleep. Dream. Tomorrow..."

But Muhammad has already passed out. As The Interrogator leaves, the fat rat pokes his head out of the wall. He sniffs fresh blood. He sniffs semen. He sniffs a midnight snack fit for a big fat rat.

The Eighth Memory
Taking It to the Enemy...

The day after Muhammad and Sheik Mahji speak to Colonel Winthrob, the insurgents attack another convoy on the main road four kilometers outside the town. This time, three of the invaders are killed, and one of the truck drivers is taken hostage. That evening, the driver appears in a video airing on international television where he begs for his life.

"They are threatening to behead the driver if Winthrob and his men do not withdraw from their base by midnight tomorrow," Sheik Mahji tells Muhammad.

"Hakim and Fatimah would never allow a beheading," says Muhammad.

"What about Ashur and Ishtar?"

Muhammad considers this. "They might. Yes, they might."

"Muhammad, Winthrob will not withdraw. You must return to negotiate with the insurgents. If they kill the driver, all is lost."

"I have no influence with them. Anyway, they want all to be lost. They want chaos to reign. They want Winthrob to act with cruelty and disregard for us,"

"But you must try to persuade them," says the Sheik, "You

must try."

That evening, Muhammad sets off on foot for the abandoned warehouses where he hopes someone will again meet him and take him to the underground complex where Hakim and Fatimah are hiding.

It's a moonless night, dark and very windy. Once he leaves the town, swirling dust and sand obscure his vision. He wraps his garments tightly around himself and leans into the fierce gusts. Hours later he arrives at the meeting site and slumps to the ground totally exhausted. He falls asleep assuming any lookouts who find him will wake him.

But the sunrise finds Muhammad covered with sand although the winds have stopped, the sky is clear and the sun is warm, even in the early morning.

Just as Muhammad awakens, he hears the voices of two men speaking the foreigners' language. They are very nearby, so Muhammad does not move. The drifted sand provides perfect desert camouflage, and for the moment, Muhammad's major concern is whether he can remain silent if one or both of the soldiers were to step on him. They do not, but neither do they leave, so Muhammad is trapped.

The hours are passing. It is getting very hot, but Muhammad must remain still. Time is running out. Muhammad is trapped. Then, one of the soldiers talks on his cell phone. His conversation grows ever more animated. Suddenly the conversation ends and the two soldiers move out. Muhammad pushes away the sand piled around himself, stretches and begins to stand when he is immediately surrounded by figures in black. One knocks him backwards, spits at him and growls, "Traitor!"

"I have not betrayed you," says Muhammad.

"The soldiers are everywhere."

"I did not tell then anything. I did not bring them with me. I am here to beg for the truck driver's life."

"On behalf of whom?

"On behalf of God. The Merciful, the Compassionate."

Muhammad is again blindfolded. Again he is lead to the underground chamber. Again the blindfold is removed when Hakim orders it removed. But this time there's a pathetic, trembling man kneeling on the floor not three meters away from Muhammad.

"The truck diver…" Muhammad says as he cocks his head in the direction of the trembling man.

"Yes. I am told you want to beg for his life."

"It would create great sympathy if you were to let him go."

Fatimah steps forward and joins Muhammad and Hakim. "Sympathy is not our goal. We aim to strike fear in the hearts of those who support the foreign invaders."

"Colonel Winthrob will not withdraw. None of them will withdraw when they are afraid. They will only leave when it is save to leave. Your best hope is the fight their evil with trust and love."

"This is nonsense," hisses Fatimah, "nonsense and capitulation."

"So…" Hakim interrupts, "what is their new offer/"

"There is no new offer. I speak only for God and the elders of our mosque. Please, let him live."

"If we gain nothing, then that is not possible," Hakim says. He turns to Fatimah. "Prepare the execution." Then to Muhammad. "You may, if you wish, be a witness to justice for the people. After all, you often speak about justice in your sermons in the mosque."

The truck driver is dragged to the cavern wall where a video camera is set to record the upcoming event. The driver senses something terrible is going to happen. He urinates and defecates in his pants.

Seeing the driver's terror, Muhammad kneels, then bows, and kneeling again chants aloud the Prayer for the Dead.

"We do not pray in here," shouts Fatimah. "We will not believe in God if God allows such terrible things to happen to us."

Muhammad ignores here and continues to pray. Fatimah kicks him and punches him, but he still prays.

Hakim calls for Fatimah to leave Muhammad alone. "Let him pray. We have more important things to do."

The video camera is running, Hakim blindfolds the weeping driver. Then he and Fatimah, in black ski masks, stand behind the driver. Hakim speaks:

I am Ashur representative of the people during these proceedings. This man works for the foreign invades who kill our children, molest our women and throw our men into prisons where they are abused or murdered. Despite his loyal service to these people, we were prepared to spare his life if the invaders would leave just one of their bases. They said no. It is they who now kill this man.

Fatimah draws a long heavy sword from its scabbard. Suddenly, swiftly, with little thought or contemplation, she swings the blade and lops off the driver's head.

She faces the camera. "Death to our enemies and their lackeys!"

Muhammad vomits over what he sees there in front of him.

Later, after Muhammad is escorted away from the rebel

encampment, he slowly makes his way back to town. As he walks alongside the river he remembers when he first saw Fatimah naked, splashing in the water…the desire he felt. Even now his loins tingle and his staff stiffens as he thinks of her as she was then.

But he also remembers her rape and how she has fallen in love with her rapist. He does not understand. He does understand her bitterness over the loss of her unborn child, and her hatred of the invaders.

He looks out over the river toward the setting sun, soft and golden reflected in the calm flowing water of Al-Furatan. The river carries all of the past into the present. The river will carry everything into the future. The river is forever.

Muhammad asks himself, what would God want? Is God, like the river, a Forever Flowing Presence, content to let the lives around Him proceed without care or intervention? Is God, in fact, above all of…of this death and pain and destruction?

Or does God want a better world for His Creations? Does He act, through His emissaries, to create a climate of peace and love and cooperation? Perhaps He even wants the war? What would be the lesson of the war? What could be the meaning of so much death and destruction?

And is he, Muhammad, a true emissary of God? If so, is it only his duty to preach the Word, but is it also his obligation to act in order to make the Word of God into action at this time and this place? Should he reveal what he knows about the insurgents or keep it hidden? Should he try and stop Fatimah or let her path reveal itself in natural revelation?

Beheading…it has come to that…beheading…. An egret rises up from the marsh and crosses through the plane of the dying sun. Then the bird is gone. The sun is gone. The crickets start heir nighttime chatter.

Muhammad does not go home. He heads for the mosque where he throws himself down on the sanctuary carpet and prays fervently for guidance to do the right thing.

It's the next day. Muhammad and the sheik are in Colonel Winthrob's office. Winthrob is drinking tea. Tiny driblets cling to his moustache when he pulls the cup from his mouth.

Muhammad is speaking: "If I take you to them, I must go along. And you must let me offer them a chance to surrender."

"You are telling me what I must do? I can have you arrested and I'm very sure extract this information from you within twenty- four hours."

"Perhaps."

"But…if they surrender…hmmm, that would be better. No martyrs. And a chance to interrogate them…yes, we will let you talk with them, not because you demand it, but because it will be better.

"Good."

"You know they might kill you?"

"Yes."

"Hmmm. Brave man. Okee, dokee, what do you want in return?"

"Nothing."

"How about a new roof for the mosque?" "No."

"Air conditioning?"

"No."

"A donation to the poor fund?"

"Nnn…alright. A donation to the poor fund."

"Shake on it ol' buddy." The Colonel extends his thick

paw. Muhammad shakes it warily.

"Tomorrow then?" "Yes, tomorrow."

After Muhammad leaves Camp Liberty Rising, he asks Sheik Mahji to drive him to see his mother, Marium. He finds her at the well where she is collecting water in a plastic jug. As he approaches his mother, Muhammad remembers when he hid nearby and first heard the old women laugh about his father not being able to make love to his mother. After giving his mother a kiss, he tells her the story of that day for the first time. He thinks she will be angry. Instead, she laughs.

"I know that is what everyone said, but I told you the truth the day your father went flying from the almond tree… he was really your father."

"Then why was he so jealous?"

"Old men are like that. One day, they stop believing in themselves…that's when they turn to God."

Muhammad takes the plastic jug from her and hoists it up onto his shoulders. "Yusaf turned to God because he did not believe in himself?"

"God was a great comfort to your father."

"And you, mother. You raised me in my faith. But do you believe? Do you believe God concerns himself with our lives?"

"For those who believe in Him, He does."

"A clever answer." They walk toward Marium's room in a house for old women near the market square.

"I was at the beheading. It was Fatimah who killed the driver. With a long sword. In an instant." He snaps his fingers. "Just like that."

"She came to see me before she left you."

Muhammad stops abruptly. "She did? Why did you not

tell me?"

Marium ignores his question. "She is very angry, Muhammad. Very, very angry."

They arrive at the house were his mother lives.

"And she will not seek peace in God?"

"No. She must find peace within herself."

Muhammad puts the bottle on the stoop.

"I have been asked to betray Fatimah. And Hakim."

"What are you going to do?"

"What do you think I should do?

"Do you still love her?"

"Yes."

"Then you must betray her. It is her only hope for salvation."

Muhammad kisses his mother.

"And what about you?" she asks. "What will become of you?"

"I do not know."

"You will be in danger?"

"Yes."

"Then go with God. Peace be with you, Muhammad."

"And with you, mother."

The Ninth Day
The Electric Cross...

Muhammad awakens empty of dreams or desires, empty of hope or faith, lost in a vast fog of pain and despair. He stares vacantly into the darkness waiting for an avenging angel who never arrives. He wonders if it is possible to end one's own life simply by the act of refusing to breath. But each time, as he nears unconsciousness, his chest heaves and he begins living again.

Finally, it is the guards who do come for Muhammad early, before dawn, while the rest of the prisoners are sleeping. They lift his limp body onto a gurney and wheel him to the prison infirmary.

The little old doctor who had seen him previously patches him up as best he can. As he applies salve to Muhammad's rectum, Muhammad speaks:

"Why heal me?"

"I am a doctor."

"But I am to die today."

"That is what I have been told."

"Ah…so, it is true. This is good."

"What is good about dying? In all my years of observing the

process I have learned two things: One is that, at the last moment, no one really wants to die. Some go bravely, some go out as cowards, but no one really wants to die."

"And second?"

"What?

"What is the second thing you learned?"

"Oh…that the process is apparently permanent. There are no reprieves."

"And this is bad?"

"It eliminates alternatives."

"Alternatives are illusions."

"Alternatives make life worth living."

"God makes life worth living."

"God…yes…God…hmmm…"

"You are an infidel?"

"I am a prison doctor."

"God is great!"

"So was my breakfast this morning. The coffee was particularly great."

"'God shall pay them back their mockery…'"

"I await his decision with little fear."

The doctor slices another piece of tape and wraps it around Muhammad's wrist.

"So. Yours will be the first public prison electrocution since…"

"Electrocution?"

"Yes, of course. We are not barbarians."

"Kill me here and now, please."

"Oh, no."

He signals to the guards to take Muhammad away.

"Again, peace be with you, and I hope you find your paradise."

The guards roll Muhammad back on the gurney and bring

him to the game room where a small stage has been built at the front. A number of large vehicle batteries have been placed alongside the stage, and numerous wires run from the batteries onto the center of the stage.

Rows of chairs have been set up facing the stage, just as they were for Muhammad's voluntary gathering. There are no empty seats. Muhammad is brought to the center of the stage. A murmur runs through the assembled guards and prisoners when they realize the man on the stage is Muhammad.

Muhammad is striped naked, then covered with a dark green gown. A long narrow hood cut from the same cloth is placed over his head. He is tied to a pillar to support him standing upright. Then his arms are lashed to a cross beam so that they will remain outstretched. Finally, the wires running from the batteries are attached to his hands and chest. The preparations are complete. The Captain leaves his seat, steps to the front and addresses those assembled.

"We gather here today to bear witness to the execution by electrocution of the prisoner Muhammad Shakir. As you know, Shakir has been a most recalcitrant prisoner, refusing to cooperate with his interrogators, sabotaging special canine units and molesting other prisoners.

"Despite his behavior, Shakir has been well treated here and we have respected his rights, both personal and human, during his internment. Whatever else may be said about us, we are good Christian warriors who fight the good fight following the precepts of charity and generosity encouraged by the teachings of Our Lord and Saviour.

"As you also know, we honor Our Lord's execution by displaying the condemned prisoner in a manner depicting the physical appearance of Our Lord's death upon the cross. In that way, we both honor Our Lord and remind those of other faiths who oppose us that their deaths will be on our terms, the stipulations of Our Lord Triumphant!"

"Ooooha!" from the guards and other prison personnel. The prisoners present either stare blankly, uncomprehending, or they hang their heads in shame.

"Before we carry out the final electrocution, I would like to read from the official transcript of Muhammad Shakir's most recent interrogation…

"He was asked: Did you carry out this bombing? The answer: yes.

"He was then asked: Did anyone assist you in this murderous act? The answer: Yes. Soldiers from the Wrath of God Movement, lead by the false prophet Alawi Al-Swahini.

"He was asked: Why did you do it? The answer: To kill as many infidels as possible."

Hisses and boos from the guards.

"He was then asked: Why do you want to kill them? He answered: because I hate their freedoms, their way of life,

Loud hissing and booing. Shouts of "Death to hadjis!"

During this entire presentation, Muhammad suffers in silence preparing himself for what is to come.

God if it be Your will, I wish to enter into Your luxuriant garden and serve You for all eternity. Please accept this sacrifice I offer in Your name—my own life, so that I may have a better life with You in paradise. There is no God but You, God and God is great!

"…And so it is now time to commence the electrocution!"

"Ooooha!"

The Corporal walks center stage, raises her clasped hands over her head and urges the assembly on.

"Ooooha!...Ooooha!...Ooooha!"

Then she walks over to the battery pack. She hesitates for a minute, watching Muhammad. Then, with a flourish, she throws the switch!

Muhammad's body jumps and twitches and shimmies about like a puppet being controlled by a spastic puppeteer. His bowels release. His cock jerks erect.

The guards laugh and cheer lead on by The Corporal her right arm twirling in the air in time with Muhammad's convulsions.

The prisoners in attendance hunker down, terrified, their heads between their shoulder blades, their knees against their waists.

The Corporal pulls back on the switch. Muhammad's body goes limp. The cheering increases alongside the rank scent of fear.

I feel the purifying fire cursing through me my body jangling out of my control what is happening why can I not see or hear anything except this terrible ringing and stars exploding in bright blue and white and yellow is this what the passage is like from here to there and will I know when I arrive oh...

Muhammad opens his eyes and sees only the darkness of his hood. But he also hears, without focus or clarity, the jeers and cheers of the guards. Without thinking he asks himself the same questions he asked at the beginning of his ordeal:

Am I dead?

If I am already dead, can I then ask myself if I am dead?

I do not know. I have never been dead before.

But this time Muhammad knows the answer—he is not dead. Which raises another question in his weary mind—why?

Meanwhile, The Corporal holds up her open hands and waves them up and down to call for quiet. She approaches Muhammad and pretends to investigate his condition. She pretends to be perplexed. She returns to the battery pack, and…throws the switch again. And again Muhammad becomes the mad puppet. And again the audience is thrown into raucous jubilation or paralyzing dread. And again, when the episode ends, Muhammad is weak, broken, exhausted, but not dead.

But he appears dead to those watching. Guards approach his body hanging limply from the crossbar and cut it loose. Muhammad collapses onto the stage.

Muhammad is returned to the gurney. A white sheet is placed over his body and he is then wheeled down an aisle toward the back of the game room amongst much cheering, hand slapping, fist waving and cries of: "Oooha! Oooha!".

The procession stops, turns and then passes down the other aisle back to the front so that everyone has a chance to see the body. They stop in front of the stage for one last celebration. Then they wheel Muhammad out the door.

Muhammad opens his eyes. He's in a different place. Clean, quiet. The walls are white. Sun streams in through tall, wide windows. For a moment Muhammad thinks he may be in a postmortem way station, a place where one waits for… whatever on the passage to paradise. Then he sees The Interrogator sitting across from him, observing him.

"Why am I not dead?"

"Oh, but you are…or at least everyone thinks you are…even better."

"How long must I keep suffering?"

"It is done. We needed you to go through that performance.

You had become too well known. Guards talk about you during breaks. Prisoners pass the latest news about you through the clandestine prison network. There is even a poem, 'Muhammad, Son of Al-Furitan,' which recounts mythical tales of your bravery. They all needed to watch you die like a humiliated clown, a puppet, a fool."

"What now?"

"You will stay in this room until nightfall. Then you will be released and driven to your town."

"Alive?"

"Well, yes, of course."

Back in Muhammad's old cell, the fat rat peeks out from his hole in the wall, sniffs and finds only the weakest scent of the missing prisoner. He looks around. The cell is empty. Little rat tears roll down his cheeks. He does not want to go on a diet.

The Ninth Memory
The Kiss of Death...

Muhammad rides with Sheik Mahji in his smoke-belching Mercedes until they are two kilometers away from the warehouse complex. Then he proceeds ahead on foot with God in his heart and fear in his eyes to betray the woman he loves.

Once he is admitted into the cavern, he is brought before a young man with a heavy black beard and a black headband who's cradling an assault rifle in his arms.

Muhammad is respectful. "Please tell Ashur and Ishtar I am here."

The bearded man smiles, showing crooked, tobacco stained teeth. "Well, that will take time. They are not here."

Muhammad had not considered that possibility. "But…"

"Yes?"

"Where would they go?"

"Many places. Our people are everywhere, Imam Muhammad."

"You know who I am?"

"I have attended prayer services in your mosque many times. Imam Muhammad."

"As a spy?"

"As a believer."

"Then why…this?"

"I fight for God and for my people. God wants us to defeat those who would invade and control our land and holy places."

"And what of mercy, compassion?"

"They are for when the fighting is done, Imam Muhammad." The bearded young man allowed himself a brief moment of yearning. "For when the fighting is done,"

Muhammad senses that time is growing short. "Well, if Ashur and Ishtar are not here, then…"

"I will have someone guide you to the surface."

But time has run out. At that very moment a huge explosion reverberates along the cavern walls. Muhammad knows it is the beginning of Colonel Winthrob's assault.

Since Hakim and Fatimah are not inside, Muhammad's strategy changes. He does care if he survives, but he is not certain what he should do. Then he realizes there is really nothing he can do except to try and stay alive until Colonel Winthrob arrives.

The bearded man has already run to join his fighters. Muhammad hears the sound of rapid gunfire and smaller explosions. Bullets are flying all around him. He leans against the rock face, pressing his back into a natural recess. He is trembling and soaked in sweat as often happens when one encounters live fire. Then a bullet strikes him in his foot. He screams and goes down in a heap, whimpering as the pain shoots up and down the nerves in his leg.

The fighting is over within minutes. The vastly superior numbers and firepower of the invader forces means a quick victory. There are, here and there, single shots as the invaders finish off badly wounded insurgents with a bullet to the brain.

Muhammad lies as quietly as possible. Until he hears Colonel Winthrob's voice. He looks up toward the colonel. One of the colonel's body guards sees the movement, takes aim and prepares to fire when Winthrob stops him. "Don't shoot. I know this man."

He and his interpreter approach Muhammad. The colonel's bodyguard keeps his weapon shouldered, ready to fire. "So, they wouldn't surrender?"

"They are not here."

"What?" He yells to another soldier. "You have photos. Check the dead now!"

"Do not bother. They are not here."

Minutes later, the soldier who had been checking bodies appears. "No matches, Sir."

The colonel turns to Muhammad. "Is this a trick?"

"I do not think so."

The colonel takes out his pistol. "Should I shoot you?" "No."

"Oh, Okay…then I won't."

And he doesn't. He orders a stretcher for Muhammad, and, as they leave the cavern, Muhammad sees the bearded young man sprawled dead on the ground, a section of his face blown away.

At the clinic, Muhammad is told that the bullet which struck his foot has shattered three bones, severed tendons and destroyed nerves. They set his bones, wrap the foot in a cast and tell him he will never walk properly again. Hours after he was brought in, Muhammad clump, clump, clumps out of the clinic and heads for his mosque.

It is the quiet time in the small unpretentious house of

prayer. No golden dome, no majestically tiled walls, no plaster friezes or finely woven carpets. A simple place in a simple town built half a century earlier as a refuge where one could to be at peace with God.

Muhammad lowers himself to his knees and tries to ignore his extremely painful foot. He prays, but his prayers are flat, distracted. He stops fighting against the searing spasms in his foot and instead embraces his pain, focuses on his pain, offers up his pain as a prayer and finds the connection he seeks as he speaks to God.

"Lord…God, I am in agony."

"We are all filled with pain, Muhammad."

"Then make it stop."

"No."

"It is within Your power."

"Of course."

"Then why?"

"You humans are not my most successful work. You are not creatures of intellect. You are creatures of emotion. Creatures of passion. You are only real when you feel."

"The great intellectual debates among the clerics?"

"A waste of time. You can only know me when you feel me. Like the pain in your foot."

"And this war?"

"Will grow worse."

"What am I to do?"

"You are doing it, Muhammad Shakir. You are a lover living out the passion of your life. Such a life touches other lives."

"With death."

"Remember what you said as a brave little boy: 'I am not

afraid of death'?"

"Yes."

"And the imam told you it was not about dying but about tasting death."

"Yes."

"You have tasted death, Muhammad Shakir."

"And…?"

"And what?"

Before Muhammad can again ask the question, his prayers are interrupted by a hand on his shoulder. He breaks from his reverie and reenters the material world.

Muhammad opens his eyes. Hakim and Fatimah stand in front of him. They are not dressed in black. They do not wear ski masks. Hakim is dressed like Muhammad in clerical robe and turban. Fatimah wears a brown abaya.

Hakim is grim. "You have betrayed us. You have sold out your wife."

"It is as you say."

Fatimah kicks him in the stomach.

"Why did you betray me?" screams Fatimah.

"Because I love you."

Fatimah kicks him in the stomach again. "If I had my sword your head would already be flying through the air, my husband."

"I am certain that is true."

"But we need you," says Hakim. "So we will not kill you." He holds out his hand. "Come. Come with us. Now."

They leave the mosque and head out into the busy street clogged with cars and buses and bicycles, donkey carts, mules, and people, people everywhere.

Muhammad asks: "Where are we going?"

"Hunting." says Fatimah.

"Hunting?"

"We three. Two clerics and their wife. Funny no? For once, a woman with two husbands rather than a husband with two wives."

Muhammad does smile. "Imam Ali, may he rest in paradise, would have enjoyed that remark."

Fatimah ignores him.

Muhammad turns to Hakim. "What are we hunting for?"

But Hakim also ignores him.

After some time spent wandering at random through the dusty streets and alleys, they approach the central market. There are guards making random checks, but they merely nod when they see Imam Muhammad with another cleric and an observant woman.

At the first stand, Fatimah appears to be interested in the melons. She shakes the melon. She smells the melon, but her eyes dart back and forth looking for something else. The vendor promoted the quality of his melons, but Fatimah is not in a buying mood. The next stand specializes in nuts, almonds and pistachios. Hakim samples the pistachios, and for a moment he appears to make a purchase, but he decides against it and they move on.

Their aimless shopping continues for some time. Muhammad grows restless. He considers just walking away. What would they do? What could they do? But he is also interested in what they are going to do. So he stays.

Then Fatimah spots their prey. Like a hound on point, she stops abruptly, sniffs the air and stares intently at three foreign invaders in full camouflage gear strutting toward them from perhaps thirty meters away. She signals to Hakim, and he too is on alert.

"What are you doing?" asks Muhammad. Then he follows their line of sight. He sees the soldiers.

"Just keep walking normally," says Fatimah. Hakim has left them and taken a different path. Slowly, gradually their plan dawns on Muhammad, but now the soldiers are no more than fifteen meters away.

"Fatimah, do not do this."

"It must be done, Muhammad. It must be done."

"I love you. I do not want you to die."

Fatimah hesitates. She turns to Muhammad. "I love you too, Muhammad. I can tell you that now. I am sorry."

The soldiers are no more than five meters away. Fatimah turns back toward them and runs forward. Hakim has circled around behind the soldiers and is approaching from their rear.

Muhammad makes a decision. He yells. The soldiers stop. The one on the right calls out: "Halt!"

The other two point their weapons, prepared to fire.

Muhammad shouts: "No!" He leaps toward Fatimah. "Stop!" He tries to grab her, but his wounded foot prevents him from moving fast enough. He slips and falls.

The soldiers fire. Dozens of bullets rip through Fatimah's body. Their force momentarily lifts her into the air and spins her around in a pirouette of death. Then her body slumps to the ground next to Muhammad. As the last vestiges of consciousness leave her body, her eyes lock on Muhammad's and he swears she asks him for forgiveness. He nods.

Then there's a blinding light, a tremendous noise and a billowing ball of flames as Hakim attacks from behind and sets off his suicide bomb.

The soldiers go down. Innocent civilians are thrown to the ground. Stalls are on fire. Chaos everywhere. Thick smoke again rises over the marketplace and there are no buyers only lost souls and angry, screaming young men with fists raised toward the sky signalling their defiance.

More soldiers arrive and they push back the crowd. Stones are thrown. The soldiers fire into the air. The crowd pulls back, then surges forward again. More soldiers arrive.

The ambulance drivers attend to the wounded soldiers first. Two are dead. They also assume Muhammad is dead, and they set about taking care of the other wounded first. Then a small boy notices that Muhammad has moved. He creeps over toward Muhammad's badly burned body. He leans down and looks closely. Then he starts chattering. "It's he imam! Imam Muhammad. He is alive! He is alive!"

That's when the medical crew saves Muhammad's life, but they are not allowed to take him away. The foreigner's claim him as their captive and insist the he remain in their custody. They place Muhammad in a military ambulance and then drive off.

The next morning Muhammad lies on the floor of a cell in prison. He has no memory of who he is or why he is there or what happened to him. He only wishes the screaming would stop because it only makes him feel worse than he already does.

The Last Day
On the Bridge...

It is the very early hours of the morning. Muhammad slips in and out of consciousness as he waits to be taken away from the white room. He tries to readjust his brain to the new reality—he will not die. In fact he will return to his town as the heroic Imam Muhammad Shakir. The more he considers this, the happier it makes him. He can do much good.

They arrive at false dawn, the familiar faces: The Captain, The Muscleman, The Corporal and The Interrogator along with four other guards. Muhammad is placed on a stretcher, and the guards carry him into a courtyard where a transport truck is waiting. The Interrogator speaks:

"This will all be over soon."

"I am going home..."

"Yes."

"...God willing."

"Yes."

"It is strange."

"What?"

"In some ways, I do not want to leave."

"I also find that strange...but no one ever does."

The entire entourage climbs into the back of the truck.

"You are all coming with me?"

"We all want to see you off."

"God is good."

"God is great."

The truck driver starts the engine, engages the gears and drives away from the compound through numerous gates, around many obstacles and then finally out onto the main road. Within minutes, the hum of the tires, the sound of the wind, the bumps in the road all combine to both relax and disorient Muhammad. He lies there in the back of the rumbling truck suspended in that difficult space between day and night, fear and flight, knowing and unknowing.

"How long will this take?" asks The Captain.

"Not long, sir," says The Muscleman.

"Can we watch?" asks The Corporal.

"There won't be much to see," says The Interrogator. "It's all pretty much standard procedure by now."

The Captain turns to the Interrogator: "How long have you been in this Godforsaken place?"

"Hardly God-forsaken, sir. Maybe God-obsessed."

"Yeah," says The Muscleman. "God this. God that. God the dog and God the cat."

"Creeps me out," says The Corporal.

"Everything creeps you out," says The Muscleman.

"Seventeen months, five days…" The Interrogator looks at his watch, "four hours and twenty-seven minutes…give or take."

"Whaddaya' think?" asks The Captain.

"I don't," says The Interrogator.

"Don't what?"

"Think."

The corporal starts giggling which turns into hysterical laughter.

"Don't think about it…that's the key to a soldier's life here…don't think about it."

"The key to gettin' killed ," says The Muscleman.

Home. Going home. I am going home. My life has not ended. A new life is beginning. I have learned everything about pain, about horror, about fear. I have lost everything. But I have gained something. We must end the suffering.

I will preach peace. I will preach love. We must reach out to each other, and just as God is a Compassionate and Merciful God, so must we also be compassionate and merciful to each other. Even to these fools sitting here, laughing, always laughing at us, our land, our faith. We must forgive them, for they know not what they do. And the day will come…soon, God willing, when they will also be going home.

"We will win this thing," says The Captain. "We will win because we are right."

The others look at him.

"Right about what, sir?" asks The Corporal.

"Right about our way of life…about freedom…about Our Savior, Jesus Christ. Right about America."

"Right on," says The Muscleman as he waves his fist in the air.

"But," The Interrogator asks, "what will we win?"

"The war," says The Corporal.

"Power," says The Muscleman.

"The world," says The Captain.

"All that? We can't even win over Muhammad Shakir…"

They all turn to look at Muhammad who is staring at

them. He smiles.

"God I'd love to smack that smirk off his ugly hadji mug," says The Muscleman.

"When will we get there?" The Captain asks impatiently.

The Interrogator checks his watch. "A few more minutes,"

The truck bounces over a series of potholes, then slows down at it approaches a sharp bend to the left. The driver negotiates the bend, then speeds up for a short straightaway, then slows again as he approaches an old iron bridge over the Euphrates river.

Just before he would enter the bridge, the driver pulls off the road and stops the truck. The guards jump out of the back and immediately train their weapons on the surrounding area while the rest of the group leaves he truck. Finally, they unload Muhammad.

Al-Furatan! My river…where I was born, where I fell in love, where I…but…we are not in my town. This bridge…it is where Fatimah and I were married…how…why?

The captain shouts an order: "Seal off the bridge."

Three guards cross over to the other side to stop any oncoming traffic.

The truck driver and the remaining armed guard secure the near side of the bridge. Then The Captain heads out onto the rusting, iron beam structure, followed by The Muscleman and The Corporal who carry Muhammad on his stretcher and The Interrogator who walks alongside.

The interrogator is talking to Muhammad.

"Al-Furatan. Your life comes full circle."

"But this is not my town."

"No. It is not."

"Do you know this is where I was married?"

"No. I didn't know that. I am sorry."

"I do not understand. Why are you sorry?"

"Soon, you will be with Your God in paradise."

"But...Ah, so I will not be going home after all..."

There is gangway in the middle of the bridge that maintenance workers use to access the under structure. The guards take Muhammad out onto the gangway and prop him up against the railing.

Muhammad breathes deeply as he inhales, holds that breath, and then exhales. He looks out over the river to the surrounding countryside. He inhales again. He smiles.

There is the olive tree leaning out over the water but still standing. There is the palm grove. And those are more palms growing in the distance over there. The fruit must be ripe. I can smell the sweet sugar wafting off the dark succulent dates...

And over there a tractor trails brown dust and blue smoke, burning oil as it winds its way through a field. At the edge of the field I can see two mud huts...and a new storage building with a brown plastic roof...

The river bank here is thick with green...marshes...a mother duck followed by four little ones paddles in and out among the reeds. She dips her head beneath the surface, then raises her head out of the water and shakes her neck furiously. Each of her ducklings does the same...cute...

A stork wades along the shoreline, her long, skinny pink legs lift and drop in slow motion as her eyes study the river's surface... then suddenly her thin beak spears a striped perch which flops about helplessly. The stork's enormous wings spread out from her body. Then with a push from its legs, the bird launches itself in graceful flight out over the river...

The Interrogator steps forward.

"Is there anything you want to say?"

"It is a beautiful day."

"Yes, it is."

"Peace be with you."

"And with you."

The Interrogator steps back onto the bridge. The Muscleman stands next to Muhammad who gazes toward the other bank.

I see a small blue and white boat. The fisherman is casting his net…

Muhammad inhales as deep a breath as he can hold.

I can swim. I will make it to the reeds where I can hide. They will never find me there. I can hide until nightfall if I have to…

Or maybe the fisherman will see me. Pull me into his boat. We could be in my town by tomorrow…

The Captain raises his arm in the air. Then he drops it down. The Muscleman pushes Muhammad forward off the gangway.

I am free! I need to hold my breath when I hit the surface. Hold it. Hold it. Until I rise up again and break the surface. Need to see where I am…Fatimah guide me! I must focus on the tree!

I do not want to die. I want to live. I want to be alive. I want to feel the sun on my face, I want to touch, to be touched. I need…right now I need to hold my…breath…

Muhammad's body tumbles below the bridge. The mother duck guides her young ones toward another clump of reeds. The fisherman pulls in his net and empties his catch into the bottom of his boat. The stork lands on her nest built atop the chimney of the house where the tractor driver lives. She feeds the still struggling perch to her chick who gobbles it down greedily.

Muhammad's body falls the last twenty meters into the river. The impact forces the air from his lungs. His shattered body sinks beneath the surface where the current carries it away downstream toward the sea, away from the bridge, away from the gnarled and ancient olive tree.

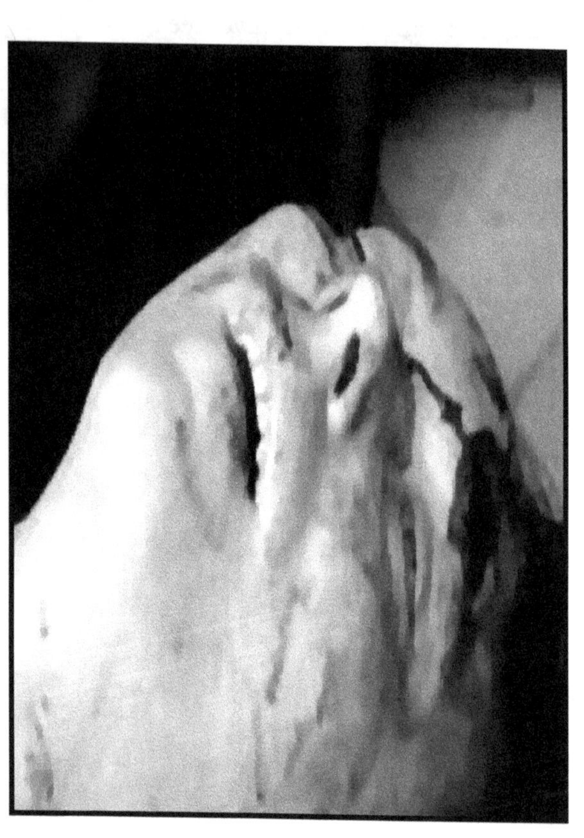

The Final Memory
I Will Be With You in Paradise...

After I hit the water...nothing, a dark void where there was no site or sound or smell, no feeling at all. Then, as I passed through the void, I entered a space of intense almost impossibly powerful sensations. Pulsating bands of stark white, then blue green purple red orange and yellow light, bright light, night and day light... Then the singing screaming mumbling groaning laughing crying snoring whispering shouting calling keening voices without words or meaning ran like mountain waterfalls again, again and again through endlessness...

And orgasms muscle spasms cramps broken bones touching being touched nervous ticks headaches vomiting diarrhea sunbathing chills foreplay exhaustion burning yearning churning...

Then it all stopped. Another dark void. Now everything is dialed in.

I am on the side of a steep, craggy, mountain with a sharp, clearly defined peak in a place where I have never been before. Everything is green, especially this meadow of thick grass that runs down a steep hill from the mountain forest right to the edge of a wide, beautiful lake.

The lake itself is very, very deep. And cold. Pure. When I look into the water I can see for ten, maybe fifteen meters. There are fish. Silver, brown and black fish. It is relaxing to sit along the edge of the lake and watch the fish dart and twirl and drift in and out around the rocks that line the shore…

There is a castle made of gray stone which sits in the middle of the lake surrounded by mist which rises from the cold water when the midmorning sun warms the air. There is a stone bridge with a cobblestone walkway that runs across the water from the meadow to the castle door. But the door is always closed. The windows are always shuttered. One day I plan to enter, but not now.

It rains. There are storms on days when the sky turns from brilliant blue to pitch black in a matter of moments. Bolts of lightening leap across the sky and then the thunder rumbles down from the mountains through the peaks and valleys so powerful it creates shock waves on the water as the raindrops break the surface in a million mini-explosions.

Deer come down to the lake. A doe with her two fawns, their coats still spotted. Raccoons wash their food. Birds fill the sky, and at night an old owl hoots in the linden tree as he scouts for mice.

The air is alive. The water alive. Nature grows and thrives. A good place for a desert rat to be when he is dead.

I do have a lot of time on my hands. Paradise is not perfect. Sometimes I just pick a nice soft spot in the meadow and lie down staring into the sky the way I used to do before I saw the naked girl in the river who changed my life forever, and I wonder still if anything will ever get any better back there.

Having spent some serious time here, I am virtually cer-

tain God does not care. I mean, okay, He cares in the sense that we care when we see an injured animal dying along the side of the road. We want to do something. But whatever we do, the animal will still die. So we do nothing. Let things take their course.

Human beings will die. And they will kill each other for hate, for God, for the Devil, for money, for power, for desire, for lust, but not for love. Whatever anyone ever tells you, I can see clearly now, from over here, no one kills for love.

Love is really all that matters. Love sustains us. On both sides, beings exist only because of love. If one is neither loved nor lover, then that is the dark void. Emptiness. Nothing.

I have found a mountain glade a short hike from here where the sun filters a very soft light through the leaves of a giant elm and the ferns bend back into the moss which covers the ground near the tree. Sometimes I kneel and bow and pray, and although I am already here and direction is meaningless I pretend I am facing the Holy City and hoping for salvation. Such thoughts put me in the proper frame of mind.

And I pray for the living. It is funny. The living pray for the dead, but the dead pray for the living. Which makes more sense when one thinks about it. We the dead have it pretty good. It is the living who struggle.

I pray for those who tortured and abused me. Forgive them, for they knew not what they were really doing. I pray for the foreign invaders. I pray for the insurgents. I pray for the innocents.

But I pray most of all for the rejectionists:

For those who reject overtures of peace and reconciliation. They will carry the souls of the dead on their shoulders as they pass over to this side and their burden will weigh heavily for as long as it takes me to carry all the pebbles in this lake to the top of this mountain.

For those who reject mercy. They will be haunted by the gray guilt ghosts of paradise for as long as it will take me to wash the granite walls of this mountain peak with my tongue.

For those who reject kindness. Their pride has no meaning in this place but their hard, cold ways will chill their happiness for as long as it takes for me to mow this meadow one blade at a time.

For those who reject love. They will be unable to find companions here who will sit with them and share their eternity for as long as it would take me to empty the lake with a serving spoon if I even had one.

And when my praying is done, I walk back down the mountain, through the meadow, to the lake. I study the castle. Possible points of entry. Maybe I can simply walk through the stone walls. I do not know. I am thinking about it. Planning. The day will come.

So, what do you want to know? What is it like here in paradise? Well, there are no virgins here, but then, neither have I seen the Face of God.

Everyone is here. I run into Yusuf occasionally and Imam Ali is a frequent visitor but they both prefer to see the sun more often than it appears where I have chosen to make my world. Fatimah and I get along most of the time although she still has a yearning for Hakim who somehow survived the bombing and remains on the other side. But it doesn't matter. We are all friends here in garden of heavenly delights.

Muhammad's body was never found, although a badly deteriorated corpse was discovered tangled up in the fronds of a large palm tree that had fallen into the river

237 kilometers downstream from the old iron bridge. But by then, the country was truly falling apart and there was no time to investigate another dead person. There were so many of them after all.